The El Paso Summer Series—Book 2

Dave Owen

Ash Grove House Press™
Dallas

Ash Grove House Press™

Published by Ash Grove House Press
For more information contact the publisher at
Ash Grove House Press
PO Box 830973
Richardson, TX 75083

www.AshGroveHousePress.com

The Ash Grove House Press logo is a registered trademark of
Ash Grove House Press

Cover art by Chris Owen
Book design and typesetting by Plaid Bison

Desert Danger : An El Paso Summer Series novel by Dave Owen

First United States edition, Dallas, Texas
Ash Grove House Press 2020

ISBN: 978-0-9996453-3-8 (softcover)
ISBN: 978-0-9996453-4-5 (hardcover)
ISBN: 978-0-9996453-5-2 (e-book)

*This story is dedicated to Mattie Mae Marx
and her mom Stacey Michelle,
her "Aunt T" Tara Kathleen,
her "Nina" Anita Jo,
her great-grandma Ginny
and her great-great-aunt Venita*

*All girls (and boys) should be so lucky as to be surrounded by
the love and legacy of strong, confident, caring women.*

November 2020

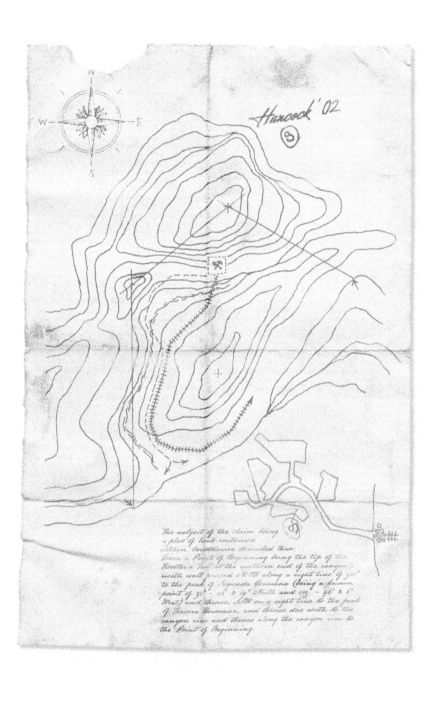

Hancock '02

The subject of the claim being
a plot of land contained
within boundaries described thus:
From a Point of Beginning being the Tip of the
Rooster's Tail at the northern end of the canyon
north wall proceed SW 550' along a right line S 30°
to the peak of Segunda Hermana (being a known
point of 31° — 13' & 19" North and 105° — 46' & 5"
West) and thence SW on a right line to the peak
of Tercera Hermana, and thence due south to the
canyon rim and thence along the canyon rim to
the Point of Beginning.

PROLOGUE

I t was late in the afternoon and he'd been hiking for three hours in the heat; his Gatorade was long gone. He paused to look back at the abrupt outcropping of mountains behind him. They seemed incredibly far away now.

He took off his sweat-soaked ball cap and wiped his forehead once again with his shirtsleeve, leaving another grungy smudge of dirt and grime on what had once been a white shirt. The ball cap was nasty, but he put it back on anyway because the balding patch on the back of his head would burn in no time without it.

"You do realize that walking through the desert in July is a stupid idea."

The sound of his own voice startled him. *Maybe I'm going crazy. Even worse, maybe I'm going to collapse from the heat and die right here in this riverbed.* He could read the headline of his discovery:

SKELETON OF MISSING PROFESSOR FOUND IN DESERT
VICTIM OF FOUL PLAY? INVESTIGATION CONTINUES

The imaginary headline faded as his eye caught a movement off to the right. He froze—but his heart raced—when he spotted it: a large rattlesnake about ten feet away. Its tiny eyes held his gaze for a long second, its tongue zipping in and out, sensing the air around it as it curled into a coil. Its tail began a signature rattle as it twitched and continued to stare." I hate rattlesnakes," he grumbled between clinched teeth.

Two weeks ago he'd arrived in the hills above the desert to check out the old silver mine. It was silver—not rattlesnakes—that had been top of mind, but snakes had quickly changed that priority. The first two days he'd been totally freaked out by both rattlers and those little scorpions that burned like fire if they stung you.

"But isn't it weird what you got used to up there?" he wondered, again speaking aloud.

He'd quickly learned to respect those rattlers. You just had to recognize their habits. Know where they liked to hang out and then stay out of their way. *Or at least make plenty of noise.* That had worked out, mostly. Except that one afternoon down in the old mine shaft. "I've been fooled by your kind before, but you're not going to fool me, big guy!" he taunted as he stared back at the snake.

Its eyes were quickly calculating its next move, and its tail was doing its little rattle dance, as he carefully reached down to pick up a rock. Suddenly the snake uncoiled and slithered off across the white and gray rocks. "Close one," he muttered, taking a deep breath then letting it out slowly through his lips as the rush of adrenaline subsided.

He watched until the tail of the big rattler disappeared beyond a nearby line of rocks before he felt confident enough to continue. Rattlers were defensively aggressive to a fault, but they always preferred to get out of a human's way if they could.

Patience and plenty of noise were the keys to avoiding the vipers. He resumed walking.

Is that a truck up ahead? He stared intently at the shapes in the distance. They looked magical and shimmery in his heat-distorted vision.

"Ignore the images. Follow the arroyo! These dry riverbeds are the only sure way out of the desert," the voice commanded. Still, the shimmers refused to go away. He decided to step up and out of the arroyo to get a better view of the landscape ahead.

Is that water up there?

"No, you're hallucinating. Gotta be the heat . . . but on the other hand, maybe not."

There was that out-loud voice again! Now he was certain he was losing it. But the voice was right—it was something real, he just wasn't sure what.

"That's not your imagination. That's a ranch pond, Professor—some clever rancher bulldozed himself a stock pond to capture the wild, rushing storm water runoff from this river bed to water his cattle in the West Texas desert."

Very clever, indeed! But what's that reflection there to the side? More water?

"No, it's too bright!"

True, looks more like shiny metal.

"Looks like a trailer to me. One of those fancy, shiny-metal RV trailers."

A smile crossed the professor's dirty, sunburned face as he squinted his eyes for a more intense look. *Oh yes—it is a trailer!*

"Of course, bozo! I told you that."

Then I'm not going to die out here?

"No, Professor, you're going to make it just fine."

He carefully scanned the arroyo ahead before stepping

back down in. As he made his way along, his for-real voice boomed a loud warning: "Okay you slithery vipers, stay outta the way 'cause we're coming through."

1

BETTER WITH A BIKE

S ummer was better with a bike. Tyler was reminded of this every time he headed down the driveway of Aunt Becky and Uncle Ryan's house in El Paso. This was his home for the summer, and a bike made things a little better. Kyle, his cousin Mackenzie's older brother, was in the navy now and his old BMX bike had been left in the backyard shed for years. Mac said once Kyle got his pickup truck, the bike was history. Tyler had been thrilled to find it. Who cared if it had several years of dust, grime, and spider webs, plus two flat tires? It was a bike! Getting to know Mac and her friend Alex had made it a little easier to get used to living in El Paso and the bike was icing on the cake.

His mom had called last month to say she and her new hubby—who Tyler referred to as Doug-the-Jerk—were staying longer in Nevada. Three months longer, in fact. She and Dougie were going to get an apartment in Reno and get settled in before they came to pick him up. That was the new plan, but it really hadn't been much of a surprise.

Tyler didn't like Doug and Doug didn't like Tyler. No amount of coaxing by his mom was going to change that. As far as he was concerned, his mom had traded his dad for a little weasel, and that little weasel didn't like him one little bit. Doug made his life miserable. Period. Slowly, it occurred to him that sooner or later one of them had to go. Unfortunately, he was the one who got thrown under the bus . . . so to speak.

That's when El Paso came up.

With no easy way to fix things, Tyler's mom had called her brother to arrange a "visit." And then when they got here, his mom talked Ryan and Becky into keeping Tyler while she and Doug drove out to Las Vegas to start their new life together. He'd rather be with his dad, Martin. But that wasn't going to happen—he was in Singapore for a two-year overseas business assignment. He missed him. And he missed his mom, too, but mainly he missed the way his mom used to be—even after she and his dad split, back before Doug-the-Jerk came between them.

Lucky for him, Aunt Becky and Uncle Ryan were cool with his situation. But now instead of staying for a few weeks, it looked like he'd be here in El Paso for several months or more. He liked his aunt. And not just because she gave him an allowance. Since Tyler was going to be staying most of the summer, she'd decided to give him $10 every week, just like his cousin Mac! And that's how he was able to resurrect the old bike for his summer wheels in El Paso.

He turned to laugh at Mac as he got a quick start out of the driveway. Mac loved her board as much as Tyler liked his bike. *Summer would have been a killer without some wheels.*

Their friend Alex lived down the street and around the corner. Just as Tyler turned into the driveway, Mac flew in, rolling past him before he could hop off. Jumping off, she tail-flipped her skateboard and grabbed it in midair. "Race you for the door!" Tyler dropped the bike on the lawn and tried to catch up but it was too late. Mac grabbed the handle of the storm door and let herself in, beating him by a full two feet.

"Hey, Miss Angie!" She dropped her shoes, breezed past the front dining room, and down the hallway to Alex's room. She and Tyler had become regulars around this time every day this summer.

"Hey, Miss Angie!" Tyler echoed, stopping to poke his head into the dining room where Alex's mom sat at her desk. The old maple dining table and chairs and matching china hutch were in storage somewhere because the dining room was now Angie's office. Tyler glanced at the white marker board with its list of all the tasks she was supposed to accomplish this week. "Looks longer than last week!" he said smiling.

"Hi, Tyler. Yes, two new projects besides my service calls. Ugh!" She looked up from her laptop to shoot him a quick grin. Just then, her headset buzzed and a little blue LED flashed. Before she could say anything else she waved to him and took the call. Tyler was always impressed with how easily Miss Angie could kick into her professional business voice.

"Missed you at the pool this morning." Mac plopped into the old ugly armchair in the corner. Usually it was buried under whatever he'd worn the past two days, as well as the laundry his mom had folded and left to be put away. Today, surprisingly, the chair was actually empty.

Tyler walked in and fell onto his back on Alex's bed. "Dude, it's hot out there!" He spread his arms out to catch as much breeze as he could from the slowly rotating ceiling fan above the bed.

"Um hmm." Alex agreed with a distracted lack of enthusiasm as he continued to stare intently at his laptop screen. His desk was a tangle of wires and devices, two PCs, a MacBook, and three monitor screens. Behind all that were two other boxes— Tyler still hadn't figured out what they did, but were obviously important for something. He and Mac knew if they left Alex on his own, he'd turn into an uber geek. Then again, he was probably one already. In spite of that, they figured it was their job to rescue him from himself.

"So what kept you from the pool this morning?" Mackenzie asked again, pressing Alex to stop ignoring them.

"Working on something . . ." he mumbled vaguely as he tapped a few new keystrokes and another window came up on his screen.

Tyler winked at Mac. "Alex, we're giving you sixty seconds to pull your head out of that screen before we mug you." Mac nodded in agreement. Sometimes, the only way they could get his attention was to threaten a major interruption. Mac had been in school with him since third grade and knew him pretty well. She figured he'd probably been working at his MacBook ever since he'd finished eating his Pop Tarts first thing this morning.

"Just gimme a second, okay?" He was more serious than usual in his reaction to his friends' sneak attack.

"Sheesh!" Mac sighed and started thumbing through the stack of magazines piled wildly on the table beside the chair. Maybe something new or actually worth looking at? But as usual, it was more like an archeology dig gone bad. And just like last time, she found nothing new or interesting. She turned to Tyler. "Did you notice that bruise on Monica's arm this morning at the pool?" She looked over to see if he was listening.

"Not really, why?"

"Shaniyah was telling me that Monica and her friend Steph

got into it yesterday. Sounds like it got out of hand—maybe even a fight."

"Still fighting over Steph's new boyfriend?" The stuff that girls worried about was just dumb and frequently bored him.

"You mean Monica's old boyfriend?" Mac corrected.

"Benji?"

"Duh . . ."

"Whatever," Tyler replied without looking up. "Why do girls get into fights over boys anyway?"

"Sometimes you are totally clueless, Tyler Dubois!" She shook her head and started to ignore him but then asked, "Did Ethan say anything about it?"

"About what?"

"The fight, airhead."

"No. Why would he?"

"Cause he's Benji's best friend—why do you think?" *Boys just don't get these things.* She picked up a pillow and threw it across the room at Tyler, who wasn't surprised and managed to catch it before it hit him. After thinking a second he launched it towards the back of Alex's head.

"Ow! Cut it out!" Alex growled, glaring at Tyler as he hurled it back, catching Tyler off guard.

"What gives, anyway?" Surprised by Alex's reaction, Tyler decided to get up and see what was on the laptop.

"Just some research. Okay?" Alex said without looking up.

"Lost Silver Mines in New Mexico . . ." Tyler read aloud as he looked over Alex's shoulder at the search box in his browser.

Alex glared up at Tyler again and slammed his laptop closed. "Sometimes, Tyler, you can be such a zit-head!" He stood up so quickly he almost knocked Tyler backwards then took the laptop over to the top drawer of his dresser, dropped it in, and closed it with a dramatic show of force to make a point.

"Sorry, dude." Tyler looked over to Mac with his hands raised and a big question on his face.

"What's up with him?" Mac mouthed silently, pointing her thumb back at Alex so that only Tyler could see.

He just shrugged his shoulders.

Maybe time for a new subject. "Hey, Alex," Mac asked, "wanna go hang out with us at Shaniyah's party tomorrow night? Her mom's gonna have pizza and their pool's supposed to be working again." When he didn't respond, she added, "Her brother just got a copy of Road Ace 3 . . ."

"And, Mad-i-son is going to be there," Tyler teased. He knew Alex had a crush on Maddie but hadn't gotten up the nerve yet to call her.

"Sure, whatever." Alex pulled a pair of Nikes from under a pile of clothes and tied them on.

Tyler was surprised he didn't take the bait. *Maybe just leave it for now.*

"Wanna cruise over to Lakewood to see if anything's going over there?" Mac asked as Alex picked his favorite yellow ball cap from the hook on the back of the door.

"Sure. Let's go. But I've got to be back by three." He gestured like a waiter at a fancy restaurant, inviting, no, *directing* them to leave his room—*now.*

As she walked out, Mac wondered what was bothering their friend. It wasn't like they never had to rescue him from himself and his computer. In fact, most afternoons this summer they came to get him and most of the time he played along with the predictable routine. There must be a reason for his ugly mood today.

Alex shut the door behind them. It was the same routine they went through every day—Alex always closed his door firmly, they'd each wave to Alex's mom as they got to the front door, and Mac would collect her skateboard and slip on her

TOMS, which she always left at the door. It was a habit she had learned from a Korean exchange student who'd been a friend of her older brother.

After they were outside and she and Alex were boarding down the street, Mac asked, "So what's up at three?"

"Mom set up an appointment for me to talk to some recruiter at the magnet school. She's trying to get me into the STEM program this fall."

"Wow, that's pretty cool. Steph's brother got in that program last year. She said it was pretty tough to get into."

"Yeah." He stared ahead as he negotiated a curve. "It'd be amazing to get in this year instead of having to wait for ninth but it's a lot of work and everyone else will still be over at McCauley."

"We'd all still hang out though, right?"

"Yeah. I guess. We probably would, until we didn't."

"What do you mean?"

"The Magnet's got all their own clubs and projects. Pretty soon everything would be robotics competitions and stuff after school every day." He paused and looked up at the one cloud that was adrift in the bright morning sky, before looking back towards Mac. "I'm just not sure."

"Got it." She thought about the idea of Alex starting at the junior high a year ahead of them. He was probably right—more than likely they'd start seeing a lot less of him. *That was a downer.* Getting accepted early was likely—very likely. She hadn't given it much thought but Alex was gonna end up in the geek track at school anyway. He was right, though, things would probably change pretty quickly if he got in.

"So is that what was bugging you back there?"

"Maybe . . . or maybe something else. I don't really wanna to talk about it."

"Okay. Fine!" She stared at the big right hand curve coming up that led to the park entrance. "Race ya to the suicide stairs!"

"You're on!" he yelled over his shoulder, as he pushed off and got a jump on her before she could execute her famous cutoff move.

Whatever was bugging Alex was just going to have to stay a secret—*for now at least.*

2

WHERE'S THE KEY?

He sat for a long five minutes on the edge of a picnic table next to the shiny silver travel trailer. Both were under a wide carport, which helped make the heat easier to take. When he'd first spotted the trailer in the distance, it looked kind of small, but now that he was here he'd found a vintage, 32' polished aluminum Airstream. It'd been the ultimate in luxury camping in its day; now it was a semipermanent weekend home.

If you were going to keep a trailer out in the desert, this would be a primo way to do it, he decided. But it wasn't abandoned, unlike the yellow one on the lot nearby. He could tell this was a weekend place that somebody regularly used. Hopefully that meant there was food inside! And a place to think. After that hike through the desert, he needed time to think. Time to come up with a plan. But first things first. He had to find the secret key that people always keep hidden at a weekend place.

He'd tried all the usual places. It wasn't under the red clay pot with the prickly pear cactus near the trailer door. Wasn't under the old cow skull with horns either. His grandparents' favorite place to hide their extra key was on top of the propane tank, under the valve cover. But he'd checked and it hadn't been there either. Feeling with his fingers under the very hot steel seat of the pink glider for one of those magnetic boxes yielded nothing.

Breaking a window was starting to look like the only way in. But that's not what he wanted to do. His eyes swept across the patio and carport one last time to see if he'd missed anything. "People always keep an extra key," he mumbled. That's when he spotted three military-surplus gas cans: five-gallon steel jerry cans with their original desert-camouflage paint scheme, their handles linked together with a small logging chain. He went over to have a look, but again no key.

Then a crazy idea came to him. Crazy, because it seemed exactly like something *he'd* also do. He unlatched the lid on the pour spout of the first can, peered into it, and sniffed. Water. *Curious*, he thought as he politely relatched it. He checked the next can—same as the first, full of water. He left the lid open and checked the third—again more water, but this one also had a long thin chain trailing down into the dark depths of the can. He lifted it and smiled as he considered the ingenuity of the owner.

There at the end of the chain was the prize for his perseverance—the key to the trailer.

3

DESERT SKIES CALLING

Wedneday morning brought an unexpected change of plans. At breakfast Aunt Becky announced they were going to the airfield this afternoon.

"So what's up with that?" Mackenzie was surprised she hadn't heard about this before now.

Her mom looked up from her iPhone calendar. "Why? Is that a problem?"

"Not at all!" Tyler replied enthusiastically.

Aunt Becky's brother, Eric, was a pilot. He and his business partner Clayton ran a regional air cargo business at the El Paso airport and flew a plane Tyler thought was amazing: a De Havilland DHC-2, which was a single engine cargo plane called a "Beaver" by the pilots who flew them.

Beavers were rugged bush planes that could take off and land just about anywhere, perfect for Eric and Clayton's delivery business, which flew emergency repair parts out to oil drilling rigs. They could get cargo to out-of-the-way places in West Texas, and get it there quickly. What Tyler had learned from being around McKenzie's family and Eric was how really important this service was because oil drilling companies lose lots of money when their equipment breaks down or goes off-line. For them, having a rig down for a day or more while waiting for a crucial part was expensive. So it was worth the extra cost to have that replacement part flown out to them as soon as it was available. And that's where Wilson Air Cargo fit in. Eric was always happy to fly a "quick-turn cargo" wherever it needed to go, but most important, he didn't need an airport. All he needed was a flat place to land!

Mac shot Tyler a look before answering her mom. "Well, there might be a timing problem if we drive out to the airport this afternoon. We've got the pool party tonight at Shaniyah's. I just need to make sure we're back in time."

"We can be late." Tyler was eager for *any* opportunity to go to the airport.

"So you're not interested in the pool party?" Mac asked curtly, giving him another glaring look. It was her strongest *Be careful!* stare.

But Tyler didn't care. Earlier that summer he'd successfully flown and landed the Beaver when Eric had been kidnapped. Everyone had celebrated Tyler as a hero, and now he was convinced he wanted to be a pilot. And that's why he couldn't wait to head to the airport this afternoon.

Becky put her phone down and looked back and forth between the two, a little perplexed. "It was Jamie's idea. She's got that big gallery show for her photography coming up this weekend. She said she needed to get a few more aerial landscape shots and thought you two would like to fly along."

Jamie was Eric's girlfriend, and Tyler thought she was pretty cool. Besides working as an office manager for a dentist, Dr. Brenner, she was also an amateur photographer. Lately she'd started taking photos of the West Texas landscape from the air. Everyone in the family thought these new photos were amazing because things looked so different when seen straight down from above. A couple of weeks ago during the every-Sunday family lunch, she'd told them that a local art gallery had invited her to have a show. It would be an opportunity to actually sell some of her photography to paying customers.

Becky looked back over to Mackenzie. "Jamie just assumed you'd both jump at an invitation to fly with her and Eric this afternoon. But if you don't want to go . . ."

"Well, that's different. If we get to go flying, then I'm very cool with that." Mac pulled out her phone. "I'll just text Shaniyah and give her a heads up that we might be late. I don't think she'll mind at all!"

Becky smiled and texted Jamie to confirm the afternoon plan while Mac and Tyler finished their breakfast. *Kids are so hard to figure out sometimes.*

4

KILLING TIME AND OTHER SUMMER STUFF

Τ he problem with having something fun to look forward to is that the rest of the day seems to move in slow motion.

When Tyler and Mac got to the neighborhood pool, Alex was waiting for them. "You're late!" he scolded. Mac looked at Tyler and grinned. Clearly Alex was in a much better mood today than yesterday morning. "Ethan stopped by a few minutes ago," he continued, without looking up from his phone.

Tyler locked his bike and Mac picked up her board. "So what did he want?" Mac finally asked since Tyler hadn't responded.

"He said he and Benji and Emme and the girls are going to hang out at the What-A-Burger for lunch. We're invited to tag along."

"Emme's back?" Tyler asked, showing his surprise.

"Yes, lover-boy, Emme's back." He blew Tyler a mock kiss. Alex looked back at his phone and grinned—he'd gotten the reaction he wanted from Tyler.

"Careful . . ." Tyler laughed. Emme was the other new kid in the neighborhood this summer. They'd all hung out that first week after his mom took off. Emme had been fun to get to know, but three weeks later, she and her family had left on a trip to France. Tyler figured they must be rich or something. All the same, he knew nothing about France and was anxious to hear about her trip.

Alex turned off his phone and dropped it in his bag. He hopped off the table, swinging the bag over his shoulder. "Ready?" he asked resolutely. He pulled out his pool ID and led the trio to the turnstile. Tyler was glad to see Alex acting like his old self today instead of a grouch.

After checking in, they headed to the far side of the pool and were just in time to grab the last three loungers near the diving boards. "So, Alex . . . what was going on yesterday morning?" Mackenzie finally asked. She spread her towel across the back of the chair and got the sunscreen out of her bag. "You were pretty much a jerk, you know."

"Yeah, well, sorry," Alex mumbled, rubbing SPF50 on his arms. "So, Tyler, have you ever heard of the website GetAJob. com?" It was the kind of question that Alex liked to ask when he knew his victim had no clue what he was talking about. He just wanted to pretend to give them a chance to be as smart as he was.

Tyler peeled off his tee shirt. "Got me . . . gimme the scoop."

"Well, they post freaky jobs that need to get done."

"Like what, for instance?"

"Like jobs you can research online and then whoever's paying for the work gets your report about whatever it is they're looking for."

"More, dude. Still not there."

"Odd stuff, boring stuff, sometimes weird stuff, but mainly stuff that just takes time to track down. I guess it's like someone else doesn't want to mess with it or hasn't got time to waste chasing something. So—they hire geeks like me to find answers for them and then post back."

"So how do they pay you?" Mac became slightly intrigued. Finished with her sunscreen, she dropped it back into her bag and rubbed what was left on her hands onto her cheeks—then adjusted her sunglasses.

"They keep track of jobs you finish and you get these 'Job Bucks' in your account—however much the person agreed to pay for the work. When you rack up enough points in your account, you can redeem them for Amazon gift cards. Pretty simple, really."

"And so, you've been doing online research for somebody you don't even know?" Tyler asked, puzzled why anyone would pay someone else to do a simple web search for them.

"Yeah, kinda. I've done several gigs and built a good rating— but I haven't landed anything really big or super interesting before now."

"Okay, I'm with you. So what happened?"

"Last Tuesday I saw a funky request posted from someone called SilverBullet44. They were asking for expert advice on the history of silver mining in West Texas and New Mexico."

"You're smart, Alex, but last time I checked, you weren't a geology professor," Mackenzie laughed.

"No kidding," he admitted, smiling. "But it's not that hard to find that kind of info on the web. You just need to know how to look. And where."

"And I'm guessing you told them you were an expert and

they asked you do the research for them?"

"Yeah. Sort of." Alex paused and looked at Tyler, then Mac. "I think something was maybe kind of fishy about the posting, though."

"What do you mean?" Mackenzie was definitely interested if it was something mysterious.

"So, they started out just wanting general history about silver mining in West Texas and New Mexico. Like dates and the counties where most of the claims were filed back then. I got the research done and posted it back; they accepted it and posted my bonus bucks."

"So far, sounds good," Tyler said. "Did something go wrong?"

"Well, not really wrong, but I got this follow-up request. They specifically wanted me to tell them more about some mining claims in Hudspeth County from the 1880s and '90s."

"And that kind of follow-up is odd?" Tyler asked, not sure where this was going.

"Well, yeah. It struck me as pretty specific, and if they were that interested in one spot, why wouldn't they just do the rest of the research themselves?"

"Dunno. But if they're asking and paying—does it matter?"

"Maybe not. But anyway, it turns out back then there were several mines in operation out in the mountains just east of here. So I gave them a little more info from what I'd found."

"And then what?" Mac was intrigued.

"Well then it got super specific. One of the mines I told them about had been filed as a claim in 1887. It produced quite a bit of silver ore for two years, and then there's nothing else about it. The client wanted more research on that one mine. I couldn't find anything else and told them there weren't any other leads . . . and then they kinda accused me of holding out on them." Alex shook his head. "It really spooked me. If the website hadn't been anonymous, it seemed like they'd have come after me or something."

"Sounds like maybe you need to lay off of GetAJob.com," Tyler decided.

"Not sure, but something about it just didn't seem right."

"So did they drop it?" Mac asked.

"Not exactly. Several hours later they apologized on the chat channel and approved the payout they owed me. Then they asked me if I could map that 1887 claim in modern GPS coordinates. They offered like, two hundred bonus bucks. That's probably more than any gig I've done on the site up to now."

"And were you able to give them what they were asking for?"

"Pretty much. I got close enough, so I sent that in. I got paid and haven't heard anything else from them since."

"And that's all that had you worried?" The story hadn't turned out to be very mysterious after all, and if that was it, Mac was ready to get in the pool.

"No . . ." he paused, but didn't finish. He just stared at the pool, lost in thought. *Had he told someone something they might've used to hurt someone?*

Mac stopped; this wasn't like Alex.

"C'mon," Tyler probed. "What's got you so freaked?"

"Yesterday morning in my local newsfeed I saw that a geology professor from SW College had gone missing. It said he'd told his neighbor he was going on a desert dig two weeks ago and was supposed to be back this past Tuesday." Alex again got a strange look of concern on his face. "No one has seen him since. Police have opened it up as a missing persons case."

"Not sure I'm connecting the dots, Alex." Mackenzie said.

"Don't you get it? He'd told the lady he was going out on a dig north of I-10 in those mountains. He was supposed to be back last Tuesday. Now he's missing. What if it's connected to my research? What if someone was looking for him and bumped him off or something?"

"Dude, you've got a freaky thing going there," Mac laughed. "You need to be writing books!" She took off her sunglasses and tossed them onto her bag.

"Hold up, Mac." Tyler shot her a look, then studied Alex's face. "He's serious. So Alex, you think the two things are related?"

"I don't know. Something about it just doesn't sound right and I think maybe I've gotten accidentally involved in something bad somehow."

"I knew you were spending too much time in your room!" Mac grinned at Tyler. "I think what you need is a good game of pool ball!" At that, she jumped into the water and created the biggest splash-out she could, soaking Alex and Tyler. *Enough nerdy nonsense about silver mines!*

5

OREO COOKIES

While Mac was making waves at the pool, Agent Ramirez was finishing his turkey and cheese sandwich in his office in the FBI wing of the Federal Justice Center in downtown El Paso. Now he was all set to savor his third Oreo. He smiled as he carefully twisted the cookie apart—he was the kind of Oreo eater who ate the cream center first. His daughter Cristina made sack lunches for everyone in the family each morning, and he recognized this extra cookie as her special gift to him. *Everyone else in the family probably got only two.*

When he finished lunch, he carefully refolded the brown paper bag. It was Christina's idea that everyone in the family should reuse their lunch sack at least twice to be environmentally responsible. Ramirez was happy to encourage her on that. He tossed the rest of his trash into the can under his desk before reluctantly returning to his laptop and the report he'd been reviewing before his brief lunch break. On the other side of the short cubicle wall that separated them, he could hear his senior partner, Agent Harper, finishing up a call with their boss.

"Yes, ma'am . . ."

"Well, I agree, ma'am, but if you look at the file on . . ."

"Yes . . ."

"Right . . ."

"But . . ."

"Yes, ma'am. We'll get right on that . . ."

"No, ma'am, that will not be a problem . . ."

"Sure. Absolutely. Ramirez and I can handle it from here." He hung up his phone before standing to look over the wall.

"Another redirect?" Ramirez asked without looking up from his email inbox. It had grown by thirty-five messages while he'd been enjoying his lunch.

"She's at it again." Harper shook his head. "You'd think you and I were the only two field agents she could assign new cases to!" He leaned across the divider to see what Ramirez had going on.

"And so . . . does whatever new thing you're going to tell me about mean we're off the Albuquerque bank robbery case?"

"Hardly."

"I figured as much. But all the same, I was hoping she might at least authorize some more hours for my wiretap investigation. I just know we're about to get lucky. All we really need is to catch just one break before the warrant expires. You know?"

Harper shook his head. "Sorry, pal. It's looking like you've got exactly this week and maybe Monday to pursue that case before the new agent arrives. The boss wants you to train her when she gets here."

"Is that what your call was all about?" Ramirez finally looked up at Harper.

"Partly. Mainly she wants to make sure we're both excited and anxious to help her be 'the best new FBI agent in all of the Southwest'—or something like that."

"If she's got her CPA like they promised, then that's no problem at all. I'll even pitch in to take her to a welcome lunch."

"Her bio says she got her CPA from A&M, so I think she'll work out great." Harper made a little "whoop" noise that Ramirez recognized as an A&M thing. "Most of those Aggies do know their stuff when they walk in the door!" Harper had graduated as a Texas Aggie—and Aggie alumni were never strangers to one another—so Ramirez was certain their newbie would feel welcome the moment she arrived. He nodded instead of teasing him about A&M.

Before he could get back to work, Harper had another question. "So speaking of our wiretap target, the infamous Mr. Anthony Fischer, did you have a chance to check out the latest wiretap recordings?"

"Next thing on my list, right after this email rodeo is whipped." Ramirez continued a slow scroll through his inbox.

Harper slipped a stack of papers into a folder, which then went into his portfolio. "I've got to head downstairs to meet with the assistant prosecutor on that kidnapping case with the pilot and the kids last month." He zipped the portfolio shut and pulled on his suit jacket.

Ramirez paused and looked up. "You do agree those kids will be good witnesses at the trial?" He continued typing an email reply as he waited for an answer.

"Sure. Both of 'em seem pretty levelheaded." He smoothed the wrinkles in his jacket and adjusted the agency-issued sidearm and its holster under his arm. "My bet is that the kid that landed the plane—Tyler—I think he'll probably make a star witness."

"Hope you're right." Ramirez closed his email browser and treated himself to a piece of bubble gum before getting into some real work. "He's certainly become quite the local hero after landing that plane." He blew a bubble for effect, smiled, and told his partner, "Be careful out there." It was a little verbal tradition between the two of them when one headed out without the other. Next on his priority list: yesterday's audio transcripts from their wiretap warrant of Anthony "Tony" Fischer.

6

WHAT-A-BURGER

Mac selected three fries as a trio to dip into her chipotle-flavored ketchup and bit the ends off to savor the spicy ketchup. Satisfied, she dunked what was left and made a show of dropping them into her mouth to enjoy. "Best fries in the state of Texas!" she said with authority, and began sorting through the rest of them for a second round.

"Okay, enough about Paris," Madison was saying to Emme. "Sounds like a blast, but you missed some serious excitement here in the U.S. of A. while you were gone."

"So, Emme, I guess you heard about Mac's cousin, Tyler?" Shaniyah interrupted.

"You met him at Mac's birthday bash just before you flew off to France," Monica added, in the unlikely event that Emme had somehow forgotten who Tyler was.

"Thanks, Monica, I *do* remember Mac's cousin," Emme said,

lowering her voice with a wink to Mackenzie before looking over her shoulder at the table where Tyler was hanging out with Benji, Ethan, and Alex. She wanted to be certain they weren't close enough to listen in on a conversation about them.

"You mean you heard all about the kidnapping?" Madison was surprised.

"What kidnapping?" Emme was alarmed. She dipped another chicken strip in her sauce and popped it in her mouth.

"Then she hasn't heard!" Shaniyah smirked at Monica. "Told you she couldn't have heard yet."

Mac was about to jump in and tell the story when Monica beat her to it. "So the day after you left, the FBI found out that Mac's uncle had been kidnapped. Some big time Mafia guy selling rocket parts stole his plane, then kidnapped him."

"He didn't work for the Mafia . . ." Mac corrected.

"Okay, whatever," Monica continued, brushing off Mac's interruption. "Anyway, this dude kidnapped Mac's uncle and took him to his top secret hideout, then he . . ."

"It wasn't a top secret hideout," Mac interrupted again.

"Well, if it wasn't secret, you'd have known where he was, right?" Monica retorted, starting to get irritated.

"I'm just saying . . ."

"Okay. Whatever!" Monica glared at Mac before continuing.

"So this guy and his evil partner—some lady called Killer Kay who wore this amazing red dress and spiky red high heels, the two of them kidnapped Mac's uncle, and . . . What?" she snapped, stopping in midsentence when she saw Mackenzie rolling her eyes.

"It's just that . . ."

Madison ignored Mac and interrupted them both. "Look, Emme, it doesn't matter. The point is, Mac's cousin, Tyler, rescued everyone. He is just so amazing, right? And it hasn't gone to his head either! He's just so, well . . . cute."

"I was there too, you know!" Mac complained and bit the ends off another trio of fries. "I used my drone . . ."

"Yeah, yeah, yeah, I know!" Monica leaned over to peek around Emme's head to see if Tyler was still ignoring them.

Emme grinned and dipped another chicken strip. "So who's he been talking to?" It was clear what she was really asking.

Monica caught her drift. "Nobody so far. They just had a big cookout for him a couple of weeks ago. Some big air force general gave him an award for bravery. But I didn't see him hanging out with anyone other than Mac and Alex."

Mac shook her head. Madison noticed her friend dragging her fries around in the ketchup, tracing lazy, uninspired circles. Something was bugging her. "What's up, Mac?"

"It's just that, well, yes—Tyler is sharp—and yes, he's fun to be around, but you guys just think it's all about him. He's cool, but he's just Tyler." Clearly her girlfriends had missed the big role *she* had in the big story this summer. Now it was all about Tyler, and only Tyler. It was almost as if she'd hadn't been there.

"Get over it, Mac." Monica turned her attention back to watching the boys.

"Well, I'm impressed with your cuz!" Emme giggled and raised her eyebrows. "He sounds pretty awesome!" she whispered to Mackenzie.

"Yeah. He's such an *awesome* cousin." Mac sighed and shook her head. Her ego was feeling a little deflated.

"So, Mac, is he for sure going to be here at McCauley this fall?" Monica had managed to catch Benji's eye for a moment and send a flirtatious wink to her ex-boyfriend. Satisfied, she was ready to pay attention to her girlfriends again. "Didn't you say his mom and her boyfriend were going to live out in San Diego or something?"

"They got married in Vegas and they've decided to live in Reno while they learn to be casino dealers. So, yes, I think he'll be going to school with us this fall." *I doubt he's leaving El Paso anytime soon*, Mac thought to herself.

Emme stole another quick glance over to the table where the boys were finishing their triple bacon cheeseburgers. "I can't wait to ask him about it at your party tonight, Shaniyah."

Oh, yeah. Shaniyah's party tonight. Mac wasn't so sure she really wanted to be there after all. At least, not if all her friends were going to talk about was Tyler, Tyler, *Tyler* . . .

7
THE BEAVER

A new security guard was on duty when Becky, Mac, and Tyler arrived at the commercial gate of El Paso Airpark. "Afternoon, ma'am," he greeted Becky through her car window. "I'll need some ID, please." Most of the security people knew Becky was Eric's sister, and most days just nodded and waved her through. The formality of showing her ID caught her by surprise. She pulled her license from the back pocket on her phone and handed it to him.

He compared her name to a list on his clipboard. Guests to the business park had to be prescreened in order to access the grounds, and the guard had to scan his list twice before finally spotting her name. "Oh, here you are—Becky Foster for Wilson Air Cargo. Sorry, Ms. Foster, I didn't see your name on my list first time." He smiled and handed back her driver's license and asked if she knew where to find Wilson Air Cargo. She assured him she had been there frequently, and he nodded and stepped back to activate the gate arm so they could proceed.

As they pulled into their parking space in front of the office and hangar, Eric's girlfriend, Jamie, pulled in beside them in her new, metallic-red sports car. Tyler hopped out quickly so he could say hi and ask if she needed any help with her cameras or anything. He *did* want to be helpful, of course, but most important he wanted another look at her Miata Turbo Coupe, Special Edition. She'd had it only a couple of weeks, but Tyler had already caught one ride in the little two-seater: she'd dropped him off for summer basketball camp last week. "Ready for some more flying?" she asked.

"Absolutely!" Tyler was still trying to memorize all the details of the little car. She handed him the camera bag from the trunk while she gathered some other items. Tyler held the office door open for her and watched his aunt Becky give Jamie a hug. *Seems like everyone in this family is always hugging.* He pushed open the door that led from the office out into the hangar and held it while Becky and Jamie stepped through and headed over to Eric's plane. As they visited with each other, Tyler climbed up on the small toehold toward the rear door of the plane and carefully loaded Jamie's bags and equipment.

After some discussion about what time to expect them back, Becky told Tyler and Mac to be good passengers. "And if at all possible, Eric, please avoid making Tyler fly the plane home this time!" she added with a wink to her brother. In reality, she'd been very proud of her nephew for flying and landing the plane earlier this summer after he and Mac and Jamie had rescued Eric from the kidnappers. On the other hand, she figured one emergency flight was enough for a lifetime.

It was meant to be a tease but after the deal at lunch, her mom's comment rubbed Mac the wrong way. "It's getting to where it's Tyler did this and Tyler did that, and Tyler is such a hero!" she complained to Jamie after her mom had left. "I was there, too! And so were you! Did everyone forget that?"

"I get it," Jamie sympathized. "A lot of times, friends, and even family, just don't recognize what they sound like when they tell their version of a story—especially once they've gotten all excited about it."

"Tell me about it!" Mac sat on a cargo crate along the wall. "Now, all my girlfriends think Tyler is just so cool. But he's just Tyler. I was proud of him too, but this is getting to be too big of a deal with everyone."

"Well, if it makes any difference, I know exactly how you feel." Jamie sat on the crate beside her. "Before I moved to the US, my kid sister got engaged and then married. I went from being the older sister and my aunt Jill's favorite niece to the extra sister who hadn't managed to find a husband yet."

"That stinks."

"It really did. Allison was the center of attention for the next six months and no one seemed to notice me. But then, a funny thing happened."

"What?"

"After she and Henri got married and left for their honeymoon, everything kind of just went back to the way it had always been. My aunt Jill went back to inviting me over to have Chinese carryout and watch the telly with her on Thursday nights, and Mom and I went back to our favorite things too, and the moment passed. Sometimes, things just seem to happen in seasons."

"Hmm . . . I guess," Mac agreed tentatively. She was unsure if that was going to happen this time. Monica and Emme seemed pretty awestruck by Tyler right now.

"Give it time, Mac. When you're thirteen everything seems

like it has to happen right now, or seems like it takes forever. Sounds like an adult cop-out, but trust me, it's true. Hang in there and ride it out. You'll be surprised, and you'll find it's a lot less stressful than trying to change something you can't."

"We'll see." Mackenzie gave her a slight grin. She trusted Jamie and figured she probably knew what she was talking about. Still . . . if one more person bragged about Tyler and his superhero exploits, she figured she just might scream.

"Come on." Jamie put her arm around Mac's shoulder for a moment. "I think you've got the copilot seat waiting for you this afternoon."

Tyler had joined Eric at the tail of the plane where he was doing his regular preflight inspection of the Beaver. It seemed to him that Eric had walked around his plane enough times that he wouldn't need to again. But when he voiced that thought, Eric told him that a visual inspection was just part of what you had to do every time you flew if you were a careful pilot. Tyler was looking up at the large tail rudder that steered the plane in flight.

"What are you thinking?" Eric asked.

"Just then, I was thinking about that little link-and-control arm that moves the rudder left and right. Kind of amazing that such a small part can steer the plane just by making the rudder go left or right."

"I think you might be getting the hang of a preflight inspection, Tyler! That's the mindset that keeps you looking for any little thing that if you notice now . . . on the ground . . . might keep you from an emergency in the sky. Once you're in the air, it might be too late for you and everyone with you."

"That's a pretty big responsibility, I guess."

"Yup." Eric took a second glance at the same linkage Tyler had just checked out. "Well, looks like she's ready to fly." Eric glanced one more time down the trailing edge of the wing above their heads.

Mac was already in the copilot seat with her feet hanging out the door and telling Clayton, Eric's business partner, about the latest video she'd shot with her drone.

"We ready to roll?" she asked Eric confidently when she was finished with her story.

"The Beaver looks good!" Eric announced. "So, yup, let's climb in and get underway. I see you've already decided it's your turn to ride shotgun," he said with his signature big smile. Mac grinned and stuck her tongue out at Tyler with a quick wink before Eric could spot her teasing her cousin.

Twenty minutes later they had taxied out of the hangar and taken their place in the line of planes near the end of the taxiway. Finally the tower radioed them to turn onto the runway for takeoff. Eric revved up the big motor until he was satisfied with the manifold pressure on one of the many gauges in front of him, then released the brakes, and they began to roll down the runway.

As they approached 80 mph, the Beaver rose gently off the ground and quickly climbed into the sky where only a few bright white clouds floated far above them. Eric spoke with air traffic control and then leveled the plane out at 7200 feet and made a course east-southeast toward the desert.

They all had headsets on so they could talk to each other over the noise of the Beaver's giant motor. "Hey, copilot!" Tyler said, speaking into the mic of his headset.

Mac, proud to get the copilot seat for this trip, turned to smile at Tyler sitting back with Jamie. "Yes, Tyler, this is your copilot. Whatcha' want?" She had a proud grin on her face.

"Oh, nothing," he smirked. "Just checking to make sure you were plugged in."

She shook her head and looked over to Eric. "Can you please not encourage 'kid pilot' back there? I think he's gotten too a big head after his big rescue flight last month!"

Eric smiled at Mac for taking the chance to tease her cousin and gave her a thumbs-up. "But, don't forget, you're supposed to be helping me look for other planes since you're in the copilot seat."

Mac grinned back and saluted Eric. "Aye, aye, captain!" She turned her attention back to the bright blue skies around them. It was another beautiful day for flying over the West Texas desert.

8

A NICE MAP

The professor pulled another cola out of the fridge and helped himself to another bag of pretzels he'd found in the pantry. The trailer wasn't as well stocked as a full-time home would be, but there were a few things to eat and drink. He'd already finished off two cans of tuna spread and most of a box of wheat crackers, even though they were stale. There were a couple of dozen cans of chicken spread left, plus several boxes of mac 'n' cheese, some cans of soup, and more crackers. Oh, and pretzels. He figured he could hang out for another day or two. Or maybe three.

The trailer had a great air conditioner, which he was enjoying even if the food was only so-so. He wandered over to the little built-in table and found himself staring out the big window. *Such a big, seemingly endless desert out there.* As his mind wandered, he began reconstructing just *how* he had gotten himself into such a mess. It had all seemed reasonable enough at first.

He unzipped a pocket of his backpack to dig out the old notebook from his grandfather's house. And the map. *No question this old map has been my undoing.* Looking out the window at the potentially deadly desert, he felt stupid to have ever taken it so seriously.

Grandpa Ansel's Lost Treasure Map. That's what his dad had called it when he showed it to him a long time ago. He was a kid at the time, maybe ten or twelve. His dad had been rummaging around in the old desk that had belonged to Grandpa Ansel. It was an antique and filled with cool old books and tools, and Grandpa's old compass and pocket watch.

His dad had taken the time to unfold the map and tell him the family story that he'd heard from his old uncle Bob when he was a kid himself. The story was that his great-great-grandpa had been a prospector in southern New Mexico in the late 1800s, and this map supposedly showed the location of a lost silver mine. The old uncle had given his dad a small metal box containing the map, a worn leather notebook, and a couple of rocks. Both the story and the box had been passed along in the family for almost a hundred years. It was all so was irresistible and cool that it had made a big impression on him as a boy. He'd never forgotten it.

He took another sip of cola and picked up the map like it was something special. Well, it was special! Two years ago his father had died suddenly and everything had passed to him. That was when he'd rediscovered the map—still in the box and still in Grandpa Ansel's old desk. Stumbling on it during that very difficult summer had been a welcome find. A puzzle to solve, a story to untangle. *A distraction.*

Unfortunately, it had soon become an obsession.

First, he'd puzzled out the real location of the mine. The carefully drawn little map with the strange doodles and words on the back wasn't a place in New Mexico at all. The survey coordinates were in the mountains just southeast of El Paso. *Very close to where he lived!* That was when he'd decided to test the ore samples from the box. As a geology professor he knew his rocks and found these to be very, very high-grade silver ore. In hindsight, he wished he'd *not* gotten so excited.

He'd read the descriptions and entries kept by Grandpa Ansel in his little leather notebook, so it was a simple assumption that the rocks were from the mine he'd mapped. He had even filed a claim to it! The question that jumped out to him was simple: What if the strike had been claimed but never fully worked? Better yet, what if Grandpa had known about an untapped vein of ore he'd kept secret . . . one that had never been mined? What if, what if?!

His obsession had led him to borrow money to try and survey the mine. A lot of money, actually. But nothing had gone right. After planning, buying equipment, borrowing more money, and spending two hot weeks in the mountains, he had nothing to show for his labor. Nothing except one very big loan to a very tough local loan shark with the nickname "Tony the Fish."

He flipped through the pages of the old notebook once more before refolding the map and sticking it back in. *Worthless!* he concluded. Frustrated, he tossed the notebook toward the sofa. But it landed too hard, bounced, and slid onto the floor. The professor didn't notice, however, because the lonely, empty desert had once again snagged his attention. He shook his head. Hiding out in someone's desert trailer, eating mac 'n' cheese and canned tuna wasn't the answer. He needed to find a way to get some help and then retrieve his Subaru that was stuck in a dry creek bed up on that mountain.

Of course, that was just his most immediate concern and wouldn't solve his real problem. He had absolutely no idea what he was going to do about his loan. The due date had been very explicit: payment in full by last Friday noon—at a crazy interest rate plus a 45 percent share in the mine.

Ignoring the loan was not an option.

The friend who had introduced him to Tony had been very clear and up front about borrowing money from the dude: "Just make sure you don't cross him, man. No one crosses Tony and gets away with it. No one."

Tony the Fish was going to come looking for him. That much was certain. The clock was already ticking.

9

PHOTO SHOOTS AND POKER GAMES

The sky was bright and clear for flying, and the midafternoon angle of the sun created intriguing shadows on the ground below them.

"What about that?" Tyler asked Jamie, pointing to the laptop screen. A curious pattern was coming into view from the wing camera mounted outside her window. Besides the remote camera with its live hi-def video feed to the MacBook, Jamie also had two cameras in the seat beside her for handheld shots.

She studied the shapes and shadows and nodded to Tyler. "I think I like that, too." She pressed a key and the laptop captured the image as a high-pixel pic file. She immediately pressed another key to zoom in and when she had the perfect composition of details she triggered another capture.

"That second one looks pretty cool. "Tyler shot her a thumbs up. He was fascinated with the process.

Eric's voice came over their headsets. "Hey, Jamie—have a look out your window—over to the left about ten o'clock. We're just passing over the ranch."

He banked the plane slightly to the left and began to drop the altitude for a lower flight over the small ranch he owned southeast of El Paso. It seemed to Tyler like they were only a few feet above the ground as they buzzed over it, then climbed to make a lazy circle around the silver trailer and outbuildings. He watched Jamie's laptop screen as she captured a few pics of the ranch with the wing camera, then as Eric finished a final circle, she picked up one of the handhelds and took about a dozen more rapid-fire shots. "Got it," she said.

"Okay, I'm going to head us on over to those mountains beyond the ranch." Eric pointed out the right side of the plane just beyond Mac's window.

Tyler was really curious about the ranch now. He'd seen the small silver trailer and a large pond nearby, but there weren't any cows or horses or anything else he imagined a ranch would have. *And, there sure weren't many roads out here!* "So, Eric, how big is your ranch?"

"There's about 320 acres—about half a square mile in all. I bought it from a buddy who won the deed in a card game." He turned to shoot Tyler a grin and a quick wink. As he did, the plane leveled off and they got a clear view of the ridge of mountains they were headed toward.

"Serious?" Tyler wasn't sure if Eric was teasing him again. It wouldn't be the first time Eric had tricked Tyler to fall for a big story.

"He's serious," Mackenzie said over the headset. "My brother

Kyle told me about it last summer." She turned in her seat to tell Tyler the story. "One of Eric's army buddies got into a high-stakes poker game with some guy at a casino in Las Vegas. The guy thought he had a winning hand but he was out of poker chips and couldn't match the ante. So he asked if Eric's friend would let him bet the deed to his Texas ranch so he could finish playing his hand."

"You almost tell the story better than me," Eric said, laughing.

"Well, I've only heard it a thousand times," Mac retorted.

"So go on—don't leave us hanging." Eric turned his attention back to the skies.

"So Eric's friend decided the idea of playing a hand of Texas hold 'em for a Texas ranch sounded pretty awesome and says yes. The guy signs an IOU and they show their cards. The table has an ace, a king, and a queen. The guy with the ranch has been dealt a king and a queen so he's playing his hand as a pair of kings and a pair of queens. He's guessing Eric's buddy maybe has a pair of kings. If so, he'd be playing a single, high pair with the ace high. Since two pairs beats a single pair, even with an ace, the guy bet the ranch based on his hunch . . . but he was wrong! It turned out that his friend was holding an ace and a king, so he actually plays a pair of aces and a pair of kings. He had the better hand because two aces with two kings beats two kings with two queens. Eric's friend won the hand and the ranch!"

"And what exactly does that mean?" Tyler knew nothing about poker and it all sounded very confusing.

"In poker, collections of high cards win," Eric explained. "Aces are the highest cards in the deck, kings are next highest, then queens. The guy that lost had a pair of kings just like my friend, but he guessed wrong about the hand he was up against. The pair of aces that he wasn't expecting was stronger than his pair of queens, so he lost."

"Wow," Tyler shook his head. "Sounds like a kind of stupid way to lose a ranch."

"Honestly, Tyler, I couldn't agree more!" Eric nodded. "I used to play poker in the army before I finally gave it up. I've seen a lot of guys lose an entire paycheck in a single, all-night game of cards. Not good!"

Jamie looked up from her laptop. "And are you going to tell Tyler how *you* ended up owning the Lucky Ace Ranch?"

"I was just getting to that," Eric replied with mock frustration. "My buddy Michael lives in Hawaii. He was just in Vegas for a vacation and knows nothing about West Texas. So, I got a call from him the next morning. He and his wife were supposed to fly home to Hawaii but now he suddenly owns a *Texas ranch*. After he tells me the story he asks, 'What am I going to do with a ranch I know nothing about?'"

"Yeah, that's kind of freaky," Tyler acknowledged. "What'd you tell him?"

"He knew it was somewhere near El Paso, so I agreed to have a look at it for him. Jamie and I had just started dating and I knew she liked flying, so I invited her to fly out with me to have a look that same afternoon."

Jamie spoke up. "So we flew out, circled around it a few times, and even landed on a dirt road nearby. We hiked around some of the land and looked through the windows of the silver travel trailer on the property. When we'd seen enough, we flew back home."

"Three hundred and twenty acres—half a square mile— sounds big, Tyler, but it's hard to use that kind of land for something productive without a lot of work," Eric said.

"But it did have that cool old trailer on it—plus the stock pond," Jamie added. "And the stars are pretty incredible out there at night."

"True," Eric agreed. "So, after seeing it and realizing it really wasn't worth much, I called him back and described it to him. Told him that basically it was land that would be pretty tough to sell unless just the right person was looking for a trailer in the desert with a lot of scrub land to go with it."

"Bet he was pretty bummed about that," Tyler commented.

"Yeah, he was disappointed, but then again, he'd won enough cash on that hand of cards that the ranch was just icing on the cake. It really hadn't cost him anything to win it."

"So how did *you* get it?"

"He asked me how much I'd give him to take it off his hands. I told him I didn't really need a ranch. So he decided I could just have it. But I had to promise to send him $5,000 if I ever sold it."

"Pretty cool," Tyler said.

"Yeah. Not a bad deal for me."

Jamie reminded Eric that since they both really liked the place he'd eventually gone ahead and bought it from his friend.

"That's true. But when I did, my friend—Michael—insisted I name it the Lucky Ace Ranch to remind me of the poker hand that won it."

Tyler smiled at the roundabout way the ranch got its name.

Out ahead, the mountain range grew bigger the closer they got. Jamie now was taking photos of the foothills rising dramatically from the flat desert floor below them. While she took photos with one camera, Tyler watched the feed from the wing camera on the laptop screen. Jamie encouraged him to try taking a few shots himself using the capture key.

"How far is it from your ranch to these mountains?" Tyler asked as he looked up to glance out the window.

"I'd say about six or seven miles. More or less. You can check the air chart if you like. Jamie's got the GPS coordinates for the ranch in her phone if you want to calculate it."

Soon they were over the mountain range itself—flying over a rugged peak and narrow little valleys in between. It didn't look like a place you'd want to get lost in, that's for sure! Every now and then Tyler could spot the trail that four-wheel drive pickups and Jeeps had used to navigate the terrain. He took a couple of pictures on the laptop as they flew over a really steep hillside.

"Eric," Jamie asked, "can you circle back around to the right? See where that peak with the microwave tower is? Right there—about three o'clock from Mac's window? There's a little valley between the peaks I want to get a shot of. See that shaft of sunlight breaking through?"

Eric nodded as he looked out Mac's window and spotted the formation and sunlight.

Tyler was impressed with the way Jamie could see something that was pretty enough for a picture but looked like just another hill to him. Eric gently banked the plane through a broad turn and leveled off as he flew over the exact spot while Jamie took a series of photos with the capture key on her laptop.

"Got it!" she said excitedly as the plane made another gentle turn to bring them to the heading back to the El Paso airport. "That just might turn out to be the best photo in my exhibition this weekend," Jamie announced with great satisfaction.

Soon the ridges were shrinking behind them as they made their way west, passing over Eric's ranch once again. But this time they were flying much higher. Tyler decided to take a couple of pictures of the ranch as they flew over. The desert looked beautiful from up here, but he suspected it was more dangerous than it looked. Kind of like Jamie's photos that were prettier as abstract art than the rugged land that was really down there below them. Tyler hoped there would be a trip out to Eric's ranch sometime soon to see it up close. *Very soon!*

10

CONVERSATIONS OVERHEARD

B ack at the FBI office, Agent Ramirez had just wrapped
up an impromptu call with Harper and the prosecutor
on the kidnapping case. Once again he was ready to
jump into a review of the digital wiretap transcripts from the
Fischer warrant. He touched an icon on his screen to open the
first of three audio files from the overnight report. The audio
app launched, the first file loaded, and a colorful app displayed
digital sine waves that moved with the volume and rhythm of
the voice. The agent who'd made the recording stated the date
and time of the phone call, and the running time code for the
file streamed across the bottom of the screen. In a sidebar of
the app, a text file scrolled up from the bottom that provided
a running typewritten transcript of the dialogue. It helped the

listener to easily follow along in case the audio got bad or hard to understand. It also noted who was speaking.

After the intro, there was a pause and then Ramirez heard the now familiar voice of Tony Fischer, a known, local, organized crime boss, also known as "Tony the Fish" to his people. Tony answered his cell phone: "Yo, what's up, my man?"

Unidentified voice/Cell 2 [number redacted for transcript]: "Say, T, how's it going?"

Subject/Cell 1 [number redacted for transcript]: "Hangin', dude. Just hangin'. Got anything for me?"

Ramirez recognized the second voice as Chris Gatto, known by his associates as "Chris the Cat." He was Tony's enforcer— the guy Tony turned to for collections, and more importantly for settling scores with enemies and people who broke their promises to Tony. He was someone people didn't usually mess with. Whatever Tony was up to, if the Cat was involved, then something ugly was likely to happen soon.

Unidentified voice/C2:
"So, yeah. I might have something for you. Maybe so—I think I do, anyway."

Subject/C1:
[chuckle] "So don't be too sure of yourself, Christopher. I mean, you wouldn't want me to be thinkin' you were just makin' somethin' up on the fly—right?"

"Yeah, yeah. Point taken. Okay, so here's the deal. Your little professor has for sure pulled a submarine dive on us. Not at home, not on campus, Momma ain't seen him. No girlfriend to squeeze. He's nowhere in sight."

"The little twit took my money and split, didn't he?"

"Don't pop a gasket just yet, boss. I haven't figured out where he's hidin' just yet, but I'm pretty certain he hasn't totally skipped town on us. We're still lookin' for him, K?"

"Go on."

"So, best as I can figure, the place he was planning to do the digging is somewhere out near Rooster Canyon."

"Where the heck is Rooster Canyon? Sounds like a music club."

"Trust me, it's not some hot club. It's a place out in the desert. Out north of I-10. Somewhere up in those mountains southeast of town. Pretty sure it's a place you're not gonna wanna visit."

"And that's where you guess Professor Silver Mine is holed up?"

"No . . . well, I don't think so. [pause] But like I said, I really . . . well, I don't know yet. So for now let's just say maybe. But I kinda doubt it."

"You make me feel so confident about your hunch, Christopher."

"Sorry, but I'm telling you, I think that's where he must have gone. You know—his mine, that thing he was getting the money for. Right?"

"Yeah. An imaginary silver mine, that's what I'm thinkin' now. [pause] And what makes you so sure about this hunch of yours?"

"Well, I've got sources. I'm no internet geek. Never was any good on computers. But your girlfriend Britney knows how the web works, okay? So she helped me put out a little paid gig for those 'Eager Explorer Types.' You know, those nerds who like solving a research mystery online. You, like, post a question, agree to pay them for the answer, and then turn 'em loose and they do all the work for you."

"Okay . . ."

"So, a couple of these online geeks bit on the challenge of locating a silver mine here in West Texas, and two of the three came up with the same answer—down in the mountains southeast of El Paso. I'm thinkin' it makes sense."

"They told you to go look in the middle of the desert?"

"So, c'mon, T! Where do you expect to find a silver mine? In downtown El Paso behind the Quickie Mart?"

[laughter] "Okay already. You got me."

[muffled laugh] "Just sayin'. . ."

"No, no, I get it. So what's your plan?"

"I'm gettin' a couple of cowboys together—guys who know the desert, and we'll see if they can help me find it. This 'Intrepid07' web geek gave me pretty specific coordinates for where he thinks it is."

"You're talking like—what? Rodeo dudes with real horses?"

"Yeah. [laughs] How else you think we're going to get out there? In your Lambo?"

"Okay. Yeah, sure. This is just like, totally out of my normal."

"No joke, T. So maybe next time you stick to car loans and funding a good heist, you know? All that good usual stuff like protection, right? Still can't believe you bet on a freaking silver mine, man."

"As usual, you're absolutely right, Christopher."

"Yeah, well, it's just not my usual. Dippy professors with no girlfriend and nutso silver mines out in the desert? This is just too crazy for my brain."

"Yeah, I know. Next time we go to Vegas and skip the silver mine. But look—in the meantime, I still want my money back. You got that? It may have been a dumb bet but it's still my money and nobody stiffs Tony. Right?"

"Absolutely, boss. Absolutely."

Subject disconnects. 12 JUL 17:43.04 CDST

Ramirez leaned back in his chair with a smile and took off his headset.

So, Tony the Fish—the local bad boy they'd had in their sights for a month now—Tony had his number one enforcer out looking for a professor and some silver mine . . . or something like that. It just might be the break he'd been waiting for on his wiretap of Anthony Q. Fischer.

And a break meant the day was really looking up! If he did his homework and could locate where this Rooster Canyon was, or figure out who this "professor" was, he just might be able to catch Tony's enforcer in a federal crime. And if it was a solid catch, who knew? Maybe he could flip Gatto to become a witness to testify against his boss.

And that—well, that would be even more exciting than the extra Oreo cookie in his lunch. *Well, maybe almost as exciting.*

11

WHO'S THAT IN THE PHOTO?

Tyler and Mac were in the family room watching reruns of *The Simpsons* while Becky and Jamie finished mounting the final four photos for her exhibit. These last ones were shots they'd taken during their flight in the Beaver yesterday. The exhibit was scheduled to open to the public tomorrow evening after the private opening reception Thursday afternoon. It was obvious Jamie was nervous about the show. But her friend Gina, who owned the gallery, had been very encouraging and had coached her on the sizes people liked to buy and how to set a good price.

Gina had priced most of the 11" by 16" and 16" by 20" mounted photos between $300 and $750. And although that seemed like an extravagant, crazy price to both Jamie and Becky, Gina assured them that a higher price that some buyers could afford but others couldn't . . . well, that implied value to the buyer. And that was the name of the game in the art market—perceived value and a sense of exclusivity. Buying the only original of something.

"Kids, put Bart and Lisa on pause and come have a look at these last four photos from yesterday," Becky called out from the dining room.

Mac and Tyler tossed the remote on the couch and raced each other to see who could get past the corner of the room first. It had become a regular competition between the two of them to be best, first, or any other superlative necessary if it meant beating the other at anything and everything. Getting from one room to another was no exception. This time, Mac edged out Tyler, who slid around the corner in his socks, almost wiping out and embarrassing himself.

"Too slow!" she teased as he caught his balance and conceded defeat—at least in this round.

"What do you think?" Becky held up one of the large color photos. It had been mounted with generous margins on a white matte board and finished with a frameless glass mounting. The polished edges of the "floating glass" made the prints look like something you'd see in a museum or a fancy art gallery. It was the look of *fine art* that buyers would appreciate as they shopped Gina's gallery.

Jamie watched their eyes as they each considered the photos.

Mac held the print taken at the last minute of the little mountain valley, the one with that beautiful burst of sunlight. "This is pretty amazing!" She studied it carefully. It looked so different as a large mounted photo compared to how it looked in real life yesterday from the window of Eric's plane. "I think this will be one of the best in your show, Jamie." Mac smiled as she handed it back and began looking more closely at the second photo.

Tyler hadn't said anything yet. The picture he held was a complex pattern of desert vegetation and looked more like an artistic painting than a photograph, which was the whole point of this kind of photography. It amazed him that you had to study the photo to recognize what you were looking at. But the second photo really surprised him because he recognized it as one of the photos he'd snagged from the wing camera. He'd snapped it on their return pass over Eric's ranch when they were flying at a higher altitude.

Jamie was watching him. "Hope you don't mind, Tyler. I thought your shot of the ranch was very intriguing. I want your permission to include it in the show, if you're okay with that. It'll be attributed to you since you took it. It's a very impressive shot—you've got a strong eye for composition."

"No, of course I don't mind! That's very cool!" Tyler had a big grin on his face. "So you're going to actually have this in the gallery too? With your stuff?" He was incredulous.

"I think it fits with the rest of the series, so yes, I'd like to. Gina agreed that as long as it has your permission and attribution, it belongs with the other shots. All that natural desert landscape interrupted by the polished aluminum of the trailer reflecting the sunshine . . . not to mention the shadow of Eric's plane there on the ground as we passed over—it's terrific!"

Tyler suddenly felt very proud of himself.

"You do know this is just one more thing to go to his head, Jamie!" Mac made a mock scowl and elbowed Tyler's ribs to get his attention.

"Ow!" Tyler got ready to chase Mac back to the TV room, but suddenly, something about the photo caught his eye. "Hey, wait just a sec."

"What?" Mac asked suspiciously. She thought he might be faking a stall to get an advantage in their race back to the couch.

"Look right here, beside the trailer. What's that?" He pointed carefully to a small detail of the photo without touching the glass itself. He knew fingerprints were a big issue.

Jamie took the photo from him to have a closer look. "You mean this little bit by the trailer that looks like it might be a person?" She shifted her head sideways as she tried to better understand what she was seeing. After a minute she set the photo down and pushed her chair back from the table. "Let me go get my MacBook. Be right back."

She was gone only about three minutes before returning from her Miata with the laptop. Becky made room on the table while Jamie set it down and opened it. "I think we need to have a look at the original image." She rapidly clicked on folder icons and scrolled through file names before finding the one she was looking for. "These are pretty high-resolution images, around 700 megs each, so we ought to be able to zoom in pretty close to get a better look at what that really is."

Tyler and Mac maneuvered themselves behind Jamie's shoulders to look at the screen as the image loaded. When it was finally open, Jamie began zooming in. Soon the trailer filled most of the screen and the details around the trailer became a bit clearer. They were a little fuzzy, but Becky gasped out loud at what they saw.

There, caught from above, was what seemed to be a person. It was a very odd perspective—a top-down angle— but all the same, it was clear that a person was leaning against one of the corner posts of the carport that partially covered the silver trailer.

"Who is that guy and what's he doing out at Eric's Lucky Ace Ranch?" Tyler asked aloud.

12

WHO'S BEEN EATING
MY PRETZELS?

Mac sat facing Tyler on one of the fold-down rear bench seats of Uncle Eric's 1982 Toyota FJ40. It was an old, rough-riding, and very bouncy 4x4 that her dad referred to as "Eric's Land Cruiser—the Cruiser." She'd been told it was like a Jeep CJ but different, but since she'd never ridden in a Jeep, she wasn't sure what the difference was. Her uncle had assured her that an FJ40 was better, and she assumed he was right. Her mom simply called it a Boy's Toy kinda thing.

This was Tyler's first trip out to Eric's desert ranch southeast of El Paso. Mackenzie had originally called dibs on the front seat for the drive, but at the last minute Jamie had decided to come along. The discovery that someone had been poking around the ranch had Eric worried, so she really wanted to be with him when he drove out to have a look. Since Dr. Brenner had given her the day off and everything was already set for the show, she'd decided to ride along if they could be back by two o'clock.

That left Mac in the back with Tyler. She watched as cars and trucks flew past them on the highway. The FJ was great for rugged driving off the road but out on the interstate it was just an old truck. Cramped, bouncy and definitely not fast.

Tyler wasn't saying much, mainly watching the road ahead over Jamie's shoulder. Occasionally, when he wasn't looking, Mac would glance at him and found herself trying to guess what was capturing her cousin's attention as they rode. A faint smile crossed her face. Tyler had turned out to be a lot of fun to have around this summer, in spite of all the attention he was getting from her girlfriends. They both liked to compete with each other all the time—and that was great. He liked winning as much as she did, but was always a good sport. All the same, it bothered her about Aunt Rachel. She still couldn't imagine having your mom weird-out on you like Tyler's mom had. *How could you just run off, get married, and change your mind about coming back to pick up your kid like she had?* Mac shook her head and turned to look out the two back windows.

Tyler seemed to have adjusted to living with them this summer. But sometimes when they were just hanging out, like around the pool or at the library, he'd say something that would remind Mac that this was even more odd for Tyler than for her.

She'd overheard her mom and dad talking the other night. Her mom had said she guessed it would be a long time before Tyler's mom figured out she had a son—a very fine young man who missed her. Her mom usually wasn't so blunt when she talked about Aunt Rachel but Mac suspected she was right. Even if Tyler pretended it didn't matter—and sometimes even said it was better this way—she was certain this had to be a tough time for him.

###

At mile marker 52 on eastbound Interstate 10, Eric took the Cholula Road exit. At the top of the exit they turned left to cross the overpass and almost immediately the concrete ended and the Cruiser bounced and rumbled onto a two-lane gravel road. The ranch-grade road headed north into the desert and the view was scrub bush and dirt for as far as Tyler could see. The desert ran almost to the horizon, or at least out to where the mountains rose abruptly in the distance.

They continued down the dirt and gravel road, all of them getting a jarring bounce every time they bumped through a pothole or washout. Even where the road appeared smooth, there was a noisy, constant rumble that reminded Tyler of those strips on a highway that made sure you knew you'd drifted onto the shoulder or were crossing the centerline. It was obvious they couldn't go very fast on these rough roads.

A dense cloud of yellow-tan dust trailed them. Tyler was glad they weren't following someone. How could you see where you were headed if someone was in front of you, creating a thick dirty cloud like that? They passed a few fences and some side roads—Eric called these little roads with two parallel tire paths "tracks." But other than these tracks every now and then, there was almost nothing out here. Very few houses. *Did anyone actually live out here?*

After what seemed like forever, they reached an intersection of two gravel roads. Tyler pointed to an old fading sign. "Amigo

Acres?" he shouted as he read the sign, trying to be heard above the noise of the Cruiser and the road.

Eric glanced over his shoulder and spotted the sign as it disappeared into the dust behind them. He smiled. "Some land speculators carved up an old ranch out here years ago. Sold a bunch of ten-acre lots as if it were some suburban subdivision. Not so much."

Tyler had never seen so much dry land as far as he looked in every direction. Their road had changed from gravel to dirt and rock, just two tracks in the dirt like the little side roads they'd seen earlier.

Eric pointed down the road to the shelf of rock they were about to cross. "See that dry creek bed up ahead? Keep your eye open for a rock gate on the left after we cross it." He had to speak even louder than before to be heard over the noise of the open windows and the strained groans of the suspension and the noisy off-road tires of the old Toyota.

"Is there ever any water in this?" Tyler asked as they crossed it. There was none today, but he could tell that its sides had been carved by fast rushing water at some point.

"When it rains out here—mainly in the early spring and in the late fall—these little gulches—we call them arroyos—can fill up with water in minutes." They drove across the dry bed slowly, bumping up and over several very large but flat rocks. Once clear, Eric looked back to Tyler and continued. "You never want to be anywhere near these arroyos when there's water in them. They're just too dangerous. But the rest of the time, if you're out here on horseback they make great roadways to follow, carved through the desert by storm runoff."

"And they make great road maps too if you're on one of the four-wheelers!" Mackenzie added. "If you know which is the right creek bed, it's pretty easy to follow it back to Uncle Eric's ranch."

As they crested the hill beyond, the road flattened out again. Tyler could see the remains of a fence coming up on their left and some stone columns that once marked the entrance to the now defunct Amigo Acres subdivision. "Your ranch sure is a long way out here," Tyler commented as he scanned the horizon.

"But we're almost there!" Mac shouted, leaning toward Tyler so he could hear her.

Now the land began to fall away again and Tyler spotted an old yellow and white travel trailer with an ancient pickup truck parked beside it. Beyond the yellow trailer he recognized Eric's Airstream from their flight earlier this week, its polished aluminum shell reflecting the sun like a mirror. A flat-roof carport stood beside it.

"There it is!" Mac attempted to point but the Cruiser lurched through another washout in the road, tossing them up from their seats about an inch before plunging them all back down with a brutal thud.

They passed the yellow trailer, and from up close it looked like no one had been there in years. The old blue pickup truck beside it looked abandoned and dead. Fascinated, Tyler stared at the yard full of junk and noticed a four-wheeler behind the trailer that struck him as odd, but it didn't hold his attention when he turned around and saw they were almost to Eric's place.

Finally they turned off on a small trail and stopped under a sign hanging between two posts: "Welcome to the Lucky Ace Ranch," in big letters cut from a sheet of rusting steel. Eric passed a key to Mackenzie so she could take the padlock off one end of the heavy chain strung between two tall steel posts. As the chain fell to the ground, Eric slowly pulled forward over the chain, then waited for Mac. She hauled herself up onto the rear bumper and ducked her head as she climbed back in and pulled the tail door shut announcing: "Let's roll!" Eric let out the clutch and they rumbled up the long driveway to the trailer.

"I guess you're pretty sure whoever was out here is gone?" Tyler asked a bit sheepishly as he looked around the property.

"The sheriff sent a deputy out to look around when I called him this morning," Eric said. "He said he didn't see any signs of a break-in and the door was still locked."

"Sounds impossible to me," Mac disagreed. "Clearly there was a person hanging out by the door in that photo."

"Makes no sense to me either!" Jamie was looking around to see if she spotted anything out of the ordinary.

Eric pulled the FJ under the shade of the carport and shut off the engine. As everyone started climbing out, he reminded them one more time: "Remember what I told you about rattlesnakes. Always stay in pairs, walk deliberately and loudly, and keep your eyes open. You've always got to be looking at the trail in front of you."

After checking the door to confirm it was locked, he put in his key and turned the lockset. "Obviously the door really was still locked," he murmured to Jamie as he pushed it open. He was immediately surprised at how cool it was inside. "That's not right—the A/C is already running." He went to the fridge to get a Gatorade and found none. "Okay, locked or not, someone has swiped all the cold drinks." He glanced around and noticed the empty pretzel bags.

Jamie followed him in and immediately asked, "What's that smell?" She checked the trashcan and spotted several empty cans of stinky tuna.

Eric was checking the pantry. "No pretzels, crackers, or peanut butter. Someone's been here and helped themselves to my food. But, it looks like they let themselves in with a key and then locked up when they left."

Mac returned from a quick survey of the rest of the trailer.

"Looks like someone shaved in the bathroom and left the bed unmade," she reported.

Then Tyler remembered the key his mom had always kept under the flowerpot on their apartment's front porch in case they ever got locked out. "I don't suppose you keep a key in a flowerpot or under a rock or something, do you?"

Eric looked puzzled and then an aha realization spread across his face. It was as if Tyler had found a missing piece of a jigsaw puzzle. "Let me check." He went out to an old army surplus gas can on the patio and immediately saw that the lid was not clamped shut. When he pulled up the chain from inside the can he found nothing—just an empty, stainless steel clip.

"I think you solved the mystery, Tyler." Eric looked more closely now to see if anything else had been disturbed and quickly went back inside to check out the key rack on the wall beside the door. The keys to the padlocks on his shipping containers were all accounted for, but they'd been rearranged. "Oh, no . . ." he said, shaking his head. "We better check the storage sheds."

Tyler had noticed the big steel shipping containers near the carport but hadn't had a chance to ask Eric what he kept in them. As he and Mackenzie followed him out the door, she whispered, "That's where Uncle Eric keeps the four-wheelers and his tools. Hope they weren't all stolen."

Eric unlocked the first large yellow container and spotted both of his smaller ATVs. He relocked it and then opened the next one. His third ATV was there, but the "Mule," his big two-seater with oversized tires and a fold-down back deck that could seat two more people . . . it was gone.

All eyes were on Eric as he wandered out of the shed and sat on the picnic table at the end of the carport. He shook his head. "So, whoever was here was clever enough to discover where I hid my spare key, then helped themselves to food, a bed, and my Kawasaki."

"And they locked up behind themselves." Jamie sat beside him, put her arms around his neck, and leaned her head on his. "I'm so sorry, Eric. That's such a real bummer. Reminds me of when my apartment was broken into a couple of years ago. Leaves you feeling really violated."

After a couple of minutes to quietly reflect, she took Eric's hand and suggested they all go back inside where it was cool and then decide what to do next. Once inside, Jamie fixed everyone a tall glass of ice water and checked the cookie drawer. "I guess our uninvited guest didn't like Strawberry Newtons." She opened the foil cover, set the cookies on the table, and noticed something on the floor. "Mac, what's that under the sofa?" Jamie pointed to something just barely sticking out from behind one of its wooden legs.

Mac picked up a small notebook and thumbed through it, finally pulling out a very old piece of folded paper. "It's an old notebook . . . and some kind of a map." She handed the notebook to Eric, and Tyler immediately reached for the map.

"Whoa!" Tyler exclaimed, seeing how old it was.

Mac looked over his shoulder. "Are those supposed to be mountains?" She pointed to a series of markings north of a river.

"I wonder if these mountains are the same ones as out there." Tyler pointed out the front window of the trailer toward the mountains filling the horizon to the northeast.

"Well maybe." Jamie was now also interested in seeing the map. "If they are, then they're the same ones we flew over yesterday when we were taking photos,"

"So what's this other part of the map?" Mac turned her head sideways to try to make sense of a series of lines with notes written beside each one. They kind of looked like one of the subway maps her family had used on their trip to New York City last summer.

"It looks like really old-fashioned handwriting." Tyler tried to trace some of the lines. "Pretty hard to figure out the words."

"It's cursive handwriting and very elegant!" Jamie laughed. She realized that Tyler might not know how to write and read cursive writing since a lot of elementary schools had stopped teaching it.

Eric reached out his hand for the map and passed both the notebook and map to Jamie. "Better hang on to these. We'll want a closer look when we get back to town. For now, I'm gonna call the sheriff to let 'em know there really was a break-in and report the stolen Kawasaki."

He looked around again and realized how lucky he'd been. Whoever had let themselves in hadn't trashed the place. So it could have been a lot worse. He knew his insurance would cover the stolen ATV, but its theft still made him really mad. Then Eric realized that Jamie and the kids were watching him, wondering what was going to happen next. *Probably wondering if the trip out to the ranch was going to be a total bust.*

"Okay, everybody. We came out here to check on things and have some fun. Jamie, let's gas up the ATVs we still have and you and the kids can go explore the four corners of the ranch while I call the sheriff. Okay?"

Tyler figured it would be more fun if Eric came with them, but checking out the ranch on the ATVs with Jamie would be way better than hanging out in the trailer.

After they'd filled the fuel tanks and Eric had made sure Tyler knew how to safely use his machine, they were ready to head out. "Race you to the pond," Mac yelled over her shoulder after they all had their helmets on.

"You're on!" Tyler screamed over the loud whine of the engines.

Mac spun a little bit of gravel as she revved her ATV and took off with Tyler and Jamie close behind. *This was going to be great!*

13

ON THE RUN—BUT KEEPING AN EYE ON THINGS

From the security of the yellow mobile home the professor watched the Airstream with binoculars he'd found here. He'd seen the man, woman, and two kids come up the dusty gravel drive in that old Toyota and let themselves in. A few minutes later, out they all came in a hurry and unlocked the storage containers. A few moments later he saw the man slam the second door angrily and the woman come over to calm him down. Of course, the professor knew the reason: That expensive four-wheeler he'd kept locked up was missing! For a moment or two he felt a touch of remorse because he knew exactly where it was—right where he'd parked it this morning—just outside this old yellow trailer where he was hiding out.

The legal consequences of his adventure came to mind for the second time today: *Breaking and entering—twice. And now—theft of property valued over $1,000. Congratulations . . . you've racked up three felony crimes!* He shook his head as he lowered the binoculars for a moment. None of that was part of his plan three days ago.

"Well, that's not true, is it? You intended to break into the trailer as soon as you spotted it."

Okay, he corrected himself, *the breaking and entering part was pretty intentional.*

"True enough. You just needed a spot of shade, a bottle of water, and a place to think."

This muttering aloud to himself was starting to freak him out a little. The grand theft was because he'd seen the ring of keys on the hook by the back door. "Strange you didn't notice them sooner!"

True again. He never got around to unlocking the second steel cargo box because he'd found the full-size four-wheeler with a 6,000-pound winch in the first one. That winch was exactly what he'd needed three days ago when he left the mine and got his car stuck.

"Isn't it strange how one thing leads to another and then another? If you'd been paying more attention when you drove across that creek bed, you wouldn't have gotten stuck, would you?"

What was I thinking?

"You were trying to decide how you were going to pay back Tony the Fish instead of watching the trail, that's what you were thinking."

He wanted to say shut up in reply, but on reflection, it seemed rude to tell yourself to *shut up.* But it was true. The last thing he recalled just as his reliable little Subaru became hopelessly stuck was trying to imagine how to get out of this jam. Then suddenly the front tires were spinning in the air as they dangled over the edge of some rocks while the back tires—barely touching the ground—simply spun up clouds of rock and dirt. It had been a maddening and helpless feeling.

Getting unstuck required a winch—a powerful, low-geared electric motor with a heavy-duty steel cable that could pull the car free. A winch like the one on the front of the big four-wheeler he'd discovered.

"Is it really theft if you needed something—but it isn't yours, but you really need it? Just asking for a friend."

Of course it is. He knew that. But that hadn't stopped him. The one consolation to his conscience was that he'd been polite and locked things up nice and tidy before he left this morning.

"Except you left all that smelly tuna in the trash . . . they're not going to like that now, are they?"

Oh just shut up, will you?

He lifted the binoculars again. The little family had eventually gone back inside the trailer. He glanced out a different window that offered a view out to the horizon, interrupted only by the dirt road that led out here. Now he was seriously spooked. He knew the man would call the sheriff.

"Of course he will, you blundering dufus."

A deputy would come out, just as he had this morning. This time though, the deputy wouldn't be fooled by everything being neat and locked up. He'd do a thorough search of the area. AND he'd probably take fingerprints. *Dang! Another mistake.*

"You forgot about having your prints on file, didn't you?"

Yup, totally forgot. That night we had too much to drink and I was stupid enough to try to drive home anyway.

"If they dust for prints, they're gonna find a match. Just like they do on all those TV detective shows."

And my fingerprints are all over that trailer. Dang! If only he'd headed straight back to get his car this morning. But, no—

he'd been greedy. He remembered the yellow mobile home next door. The one that looked abandoned. He'd decided to check it out. And sure enough, he'd found plenty of food in here to stuff his backpack.

"But you took too long, didn't you? You're such a nit!"

How was I to know the sheriff would be coming by? Before he could leave, he'd heard a car on the gravel road. And not just any car. It was a black and white sheriff's SUV. Then a sheriff's deputy got out and made his way up the long drive to the Airstream—the Airstream he'd just left! He hadn't spent a lot of time looking around. The door was locked; the container was locked. He was only out of his Tahoe ten minutes.

"But he didn't leave, did he?"

No. He'd sat there in his SUV for over an hour talking to someone, typing on his laptop. Maybe his dispatcher, maybe his wife. Who knows?

"And all you could do was watch."

Yup, all I could do was watch. When the deputy finally turned the black-and-white around and headed off, he should have bolted for the door—right then.

"But no, you took your time, didn't you?"

Correct again. Too much time! Who knew some little family would show up at the Airstream in an old Landcruiser? And now—he was trapped again!

He noticed movement once more over at the trailer. They weren't leaving. They were getting three quad runners out of the other storage unit and soon three of them headed off toward the big pond. But the man hadn't gone with them—he'd gotten on his phone after the others had left and in a few moments was having an animated conversation, walking around and pointing to the storage containers while he talked. *As if the sheriff's dispatcher could see him.* If he was reporting the break-in and theft, then the sheriff would send a deputy back.

"You won't just be stuck, you'll be caught." He scanned the property, trying to spot the riders on their noisy four-runners.

"You know, it's a long shot, but if you take off just as soon as the man steps inside, the noise of the Kawasaki might not be noticed. It might be your only option." This time the voice made sense.

The man at the Airstream looked down at his mobile phone and ended his call. He put the phone in his back pocket as he looked around and then walked back to the trailer. Just as he reached for the door handle of the Airstream, the professor slipped out and climbed on the Kawasaki. He started it up, and headed out across the yard to the west, hoping he didn't raise any attention.

He knew his problems were about to get worse. He had to get to the mountains without drawing too much attention and get his car free. But his bigger problem was going to be how to slip back into El Paso without Tony the Fish knowing. With the heat of the afternoon sun beating down he tried to calm his fears and focus on the desert ahead of him.

"First things first and one thing at a time!" his voice told him. *Yes. One thing at a time.*

14

THE RIDE BACK

I t was after lunch and starting to push two p.m. when the Cruiser finally turned off the dusty ranch road and rolled onto the asphalt of the highway overpass. As they accelerated down the ramp and onto the interstate, Tyler looked back to trace the little gravel road as far as he could before it disappeared from sight. It occurred to him just how *much* there was *out there*—out beyond the view of your car window when you were buzzing down an interstate highway at seventy or so miles an hour.

He continued to stare out the back window as the overpass shrank from view. How many cars drove under that bridge every day? None of them knew—or cared—that ten miles or so out into the desert there was a little ranch with a trailer and a stock pond and a collection of quad runners in a storage unit. *And rattlesnakes!* At least that's what Eric claimed. But they hadn't seen a single one all day.

Tyler turned his attention back to the front seat. He was kind of glad Jamie had the front seat and not him. He wasn't a big fan of looking into the glare of the sun when driving west. The sun was too intense out here in Texas. He glanced at Mac across from him in the back of the Land Cruiser. She was in her own world for now, reading the latest issue of some girls' magazine on her iPad. He looked through the window beyond her watching as the brown and tan landscape rolled along with its occasional interruptions of green splotches—some kind of plant that was struggling to grow in the desert—and tried to imagine what they'd look like in an aerial photograph from 7000 feet above.

Most of his life he'd lived in Overland Park on the outskirts of Kansas City. *There were lots of trees there.* Everything that came to mind back there seemed green. Green grass, green trees, green woods, and green hills. Several times this past week he'd caught himself thinking about KC. He'd been gone only six or seven weeks so far, but it seemed so much longer ago that Doug-the-jerk had driven him and his mom to El Paso—*in his dad's car*. It was starting to feel like he'd left home over a year ago. It struck him that how long ago something happened maybe felt different depending on how much you did or didn't like whatever it was you were doing now. *Or something like that.*

A lot had happened since his mom took off. At thoughtful times like this he realized he still missed her. But what he really missed was how he and his dad and mom had all had so much fun before everything got so tense. Lately he'd figured out those fun times were really a lot further back than he used to think they were. By the time his mom told his dad that she was glad he was leaving for Singapore and he shouldn't bother to come home . . . well, things had already been tense for a long time. He could see that now.

And even though he and his mom had to move to that nasty little apartment and he'd changed schools when she sold the house, it had still been he and his mom, and that had been sort of okay. He hadn't liked his new school much and he still missed his dad, but he and his mom were okay when it was just the two of them. But that changed totally when Doug-the-jerk dropped into his mom's life and completely ruined everything! He knew that thinking too much about mom's boyfriend Doug—*no, wait, her husband Doug*—and about how everything had changed between him and his mom would only make him angry. But lately he'd figured out that instead of just getting mad, he could switch over and think about something else—like about the great time he'd had at the ranch today! *Better than getting frustrated about Doug.*

His mind wandered back to snakes. He really had hoped to see one today—maybe a big old six-foot rattlesnake! That would have been scary but amazing. But that hadn't happened. And then as he thought about it, he decided he was glad they hadn't found one. *At least not this time.* If they *had* seen one, he might have jumped and run the other direction and then Mac probably would have laughed at him. Or who knows? Maybe *she'd* have screamed and run away first. Hard to know what you'd really do if you saw a rattler up close.

He glanced again toward Mac, still scrolling through pictures and stories on her tablet. He smiled and looked back out the window. He'd been really lucky to land with Uncle Ryan and Aunt Becky. And with Mac. When his mom drove away with Doug two months ago he'd felt angry and abandoned at being dumped off in El Paso. But as it turned out, Mac was pretty fun to hang out with, and he also really liked her best friend, Alex. In fact, he figured Alex was really *his* best friend now. And it was also pretty cool that Mac's uncle was a pilot and that he and his fiancée, Jamie, took him and Mac on some pretty awesome adventures with them. Especially when they got to go flying in Eric's plane.

As he continued watching the scenery, Tyler thought about the afternoon. Four-wheeling on the quad runners had been great, but he felt bad for Eric with that break-in and the stolen Kawasaki. But he'd handled it all pretty well—he was been pretty upbeat by the time they'd loaded up the Cruiser for the ride home.

A sheriff's deputy had come out to file a report. Since the theft was valued at over $1000, the county crime scene unit had taken fingerprints and photos. *Just like they do on TV!* The deputy told Eric and Jamie that solving a rural break-in like this was a long shot. Sometimes, if it'd been done by older kids who'd already been in trouble with the law, they might get a break and find who did it and recover what had been stolen. But since whoever had broken into the trailer had not only locked the storage unit after stealing the Kawasaki, but had also locked up the house—well, that sounded like some professional thief who knew what they were doing, not a couple of kids. He'd said the fingerprints were the wild card in solving crimes like these. Sometimes they ran a set of prints and found a match from something that had happened years ago and could almost immediately identify a suspect. You just never knew what might turn up.

The bouncy ride in the back of the Cruiser and the rhythm of the passing landscape was making Tyler drowsy. The excitement of the day slipped below his consciousness and he fell asleep, with scenes of Kansas City drifting in and out of his dreams. The next thing he knew, they were pulling into the driveway and Mac was getting ready to squirt him with a water bottle to wake him up. Peeking out from under his almost closed eyelids he spotted the danger just in time and suddenly reached out and snatched the bottle from her. She was surprised, but it brought a big laugh and a tough, playful smack of her fist on his arm.

Close call.

15

INTREPID07

"Can you believe someone would steal one of my photos from the gallery?" Jamie asked Becky as she set down her purse then went to the coffee station and started brewing herself a K-Cup of jasmine tea.

Mac and Tyler were at the counter with Alex. When he'd showed up, they'd decided to have a second round of breakfast. "Which picture?" Tyler mumbled, his mouth full of Cheerios.

"That really cool one up in the mountains. The one I thought would be the best in the show. I just can't believe someone could be so bold as to take it off the wall and walk out the door with it!"

"Seriously?" Becky set down the glass she'd unloaded from the dishwasher. She located her most recent cup of coffee and put it in the microwave to reheat it.

Alex looked up from his bowl of Cinnamon Chex. "Did the

gallery have any minicams that might have caught the theft?" He played with his spoon before taking another bite as he watched Jamie closely. He was ready for a major conspiracy.

"Gina found some footage on her security system's hard drive. She had two cameras that caught the theft but neither one showed the person's face."

"When did this happen?" Becky set Jamie's tea in front of her and then retrieved her coffee from the microwave and joined her at the table.

"Thanks." Jamie squirted some honey into the warm brew, stirred it, and took a sip.

"The time stamp on the footage shows it was around 5:30 this morning. The person unlocks the front door of the gallery, goes straight to the photo, carefully lifts it from the wall then heads back out through the door with it under their arm, and the door closes. The exterior camera shows the person locking the door and then they turn and leave."

"And no alarm?" Alex asked, still sorting pieces of cereal to each side of the bowl with his spoon.

"Well, yes—but since the door was actually unlocked with a key, the alarm gives you sixty seconds to punch in the entry code before it goes off. The thief was in and out in less than forty-five. It looks like whoever they were, they just wanted *that* particular picture. In and back out in less than a minute . . . I bet they were halfway down the street before the alarm even sounded."

Alex stirred his cereal back from the edges and took another bite. "Where did you say the picture was taken?" He began messing with his spoon again.

"Up in the mountains north of Eric's ranch," Mac answered. "We flew over them when we went flying with Eric and Jamie a couple of days ago."

"Oh, yeah," Alex pointed his spoon for emphasis. "That was the same batch where you thought you saw some guy at Eric's trailer, right?"

"No," Mac corrected him, "we *DID* see someone at Eric's trailer."

"Have you got your laptop with you, Jamie?" Tyler was curious to have a closer look at the photo.

"Out in the trunk of the Miata." She reached into the pocket of her jeans, pulled out the key, and tossed it to Tyler.

"Be right back!" He caught the key fob and headed for the door.

"So in the meantime, have you sold any of your other prints yet?" Becky asked.

"Several lookers yesterday—I guess quite a few, really. One couple bought two during the reception and then three more later in the evening. I guess that's not too bad for a first day."

"Sounds like some serious sales, given the prices." Becky raised her eyebrows, impressed, then took another sip of her coffee.

"So these are those aerial photos you were telling me about?" Alex asked Mac. "The ones that look straight down and kinda look like abstract geometric shapes?"

"Yup. Most of them are pretty cool. Some of them are really a challenge when you first look at them. It sort of takes a while to figure out exactly what you're seeing."

"Kinda like those pictures from the space shuttle and the space station, right?"

"Exactly, Alex," Jamie smiled. "In fact, I studied quite a few space photographs before getting started. I needed a better idea of how our brain tries to decipher geometric objects. Many things you recognize from a normal vantage point on the ground look totally unfamiliar from above."

Tyler came back with Jamie's laptop. "Here you go." He set it down and handed her the keys.

Jamie soon had the photo file of the stolen picture on her screen. Alex left his spoon in the bowl and came over for a closer look. He wrinkled his eyebrows as he turned the laptop for a closer look and started manipulating the image, then zoomed in. When he'd finished looking, he returned to the counter and helped himself to a second bowl of Cinnamon Chex.

"What's up?" Tyler kept his eyes on Alex. "I've seen that look before."

"I know where that is," Alex said simply.

"Well of course, you know where it is," Mac retorted, exasperated with her friend. "I just told you where it was five minutes ago."

"No," he said, shaking his head. "No, I mean I know exactly where that is." Alex took another bite of cereal, then pointed to the laptop with his spoon. Everyone watched Alex, waiting for him to explain, but he milked the moment before finally swallowing his mouthful and filling them in on what he knew and how.

"You remember when you came over Monday and I was busy and you wouldn't leave me alone and I told you I was working on a job posting?"

"You mean something about silver mines?" Tyler asked, playing along. "You're talking about that online gig you were so worried about?"

"Right, my online research as *Intrepid07*."

"What online gig?" Becky gave Mackenzie the "Mom-Eye."

"Yeah, what are we talking about?" Jamie was suddenly very curious.

"Alex does online research for some website called GetAJob. com," Tyler responded. "He was telling us the other day about a job where the client was asking about an old silver mine."

Alex smiled and nodded, basking at being the center of

attention. "So the center of that photo of yours . . . that's exactly where that silver mine is that I told you about." He walked back to the laptop and opened a browser screen beside the photo. A few clicks later he had a satellite map of the same location right alongside Jamie's photo. Slightly different angles but clearly the same place. "The Gunther-Morrison Claim of 1889," he announced. "Up in the little mountain range just southeast of here."

Jamie looked puzzled for a moment, then reached into her handbag to pull out the notebook and map Tyler had found on the floor at Eric's trailer and placed them on the counter in front of Alex. "Mac and Tyler can give you the backstory on these, but I recall there was something in here about a Gunther somebody." She watched as Alex quickly thumbed through the notebook. The cover page had an inscription in ink, written in very fancy penmanship: *Personal property of Luther Gunther, Esq.—RR #4; Burnet, Texas.*

"Impressive." Alex put the notebook on the counter and unfolded the map. He puzzled over it for a couple of minutes before looking back up. "You found these at the trailer where the break-in happened?" he finally asked, looking at Tyler and Mac.

"Yup. I'm pretty sure whoever was helping themselves to Eric's trailer left them behind," Mac replied. "Or, maybe they fell out of a pocket or backpack or something. Either way, doesn't look like something you'd leave on purpose."

"When I looked at it, I thought it looked like a map to find a silver mine." Tyler watched Alex closely. "What are you thinking?"

Alex went back to look at the aerial map on the laptop and compared it again to Jamie's photo. "Well, it looks like it's probably the same place as that silver mine I was helping my client with." He stood up and looked over at Jamie. "And I'm not an expert, but it looks like the notes in the book are the kind of notes a person would make if they were testing for evidence of silver. The kind of notes you'd use to make a silver claim."

Everyone was silent for a moment as they considered Alex's conclusions.

"You said you'd located a Gunther-Morrison claim in your research?" Jamie asked.

"Yeah. So it makes sense that Mr. Luther Gunther—who must have kept his notes in this book—was probably one of the partners named in the Gunther-Morrison Claim. That was the mine I was researching. This notebook was probably his field notes and the map would have been used to document his claim back in the 1880s.

"So it's a map to a lost silver mine?" Mac was getting excited.

"Not exactly." Alex shook his head. He opened the old leather notebook, turned to one of the last entries, and pointed to the date. "Whoever kept notes in this book was doing it in '88." Alex paused and then clarified: "That's like the year – 1888."

"So these notes would have been made during an initial field survey. Is that what you're saying?" Jamie asked, answering her own question.

"Pretty much," Alex nodded. "And then either this guy—or someone he leased the claim to—came along a year or so later and ran a very successful mine. That's what I found online. I think it was in operation from 1889 until 1892. After the silver ore played out, it was abandoned."

"Which means this is a map to a mine that has already been mined." Jamie turned to look out the window as she tried to figure out where this all might be going.

"And that means this isn't a lost treasure map," Mac sighed with a touch of disappointment.

Tyler picked up the map for another look. Suddenly puzzled,

he set the map down where Alex could see it. "Look up here in the corner," Tyler pointed to a very small note written in faint pencil near the edge of the map along with the letter *s* in a circle. "Hancock '02 . . . what does that mean?"

"What about it?" Mac perked up, her sense of a mystery back in full force.

"Well, suppose '02 means 1902?" Tyler mused. "But if the mine was all out of silver and abandoned after 1892, why would somebody make a note on the map ten years later in 1902? It doesn't make any sense, does it?"

Alex was intrigued and pulled the map closer. "Hmm . . . I see what you mean." He turned the map sideways for a better look. "And look over here, in this smaller drawing below the map. There's another letter *s* just like the other one—and it's also written in pencil with a circle around it."

Jamie leaned over for a look while Becky came around as well. It was getting pretty crowded around the corner of the kitchen island.

"Did you notice something different about the sketch?" Jamie smiled and went back and took another sip of tea.

"What are you seeing?" Becky asked, still looking over the kids' shoulders.

"Look at the ink. The odd little sketch at the bottom of the map where Alex noticed the second letter *s*—it probably wasn't a part of the original document."

"What do you mean?" Mac asked.

"Whoever drew that side sketch used a dark, greenish ink using a broad-tip pen. Probably a fountain pen. But the original map was drawn by a person who really knew how to draw a map. It had fine, careful lines in black ink made with the fine-tip nib of a drafting pen.

"You're right," Alex agreed slowly, after taking another look.

He was about to set the map down again, but stopped and turned it over. "Hang on . . . look at this weird verse on the back. Makes no sense, but it's written in that same green ink."

Becky reached across and picked up the map. After looking it over, she read the verse aloud:

When shall we three meet again
In thunder, lightning, or in rain?
When the hurly-burly's done,
When the battle's lost and won.
That will be ere the set of sun.
Where the place?
Upon the heath.

"That's just plain nuts." Mac shook her head at the odd sounding words.

"No," her mom replied, looking up, "it's Shakespeare. It's the opening speech from *Macbeth*," she said confidently. "The conversation of the three witches that opens one of his most famous plays."

"Mom was an English major in college," Mac explained when she noticed the look of surprise on Tyler's and Alex's faces. "She taught high school writing and literature."

Becky suddenly blushed and grinned, which surprised her. It was nice to be noticed for a change as someone who knew more than just how to fix supper. She reread the entry. "Well, the verses are from *Macbeth*, but the stuff under it just looks like an odd collection of letters arranged to look like sentences." Now everybody took turns looking more closely at what had been written on the back of the map: *Cdbgb akad cdbgb bogd labg nc0h ata0d vgz. Azda akad azda uegd azeb axgd maj0b wld0c. cnl azeb miid atdc wlji ajec vtr. Dcpbh atdc qoh atdc xcdc ajec bbtah.*

"Looks like some foreign language. In fact, it almost looks Irish or Celtic, but it's not." Jamie passed the map and verse back to Alex.

Suddenly, it occurred to Alex what he was looking at, "Oh my gosh! I think we've got a book key cryptogram staring us in the face."

"A what?" Becky asked.

"What's a key-book cryptograph?" Mac echoed.

"Cryptogram," Alex corrected, "a book key cryptogram. It's a set of coded letters that represent words. Impossible to solve unless you have a copy of the same book that the code was based on. Or a very powerful supercomputer."

"Dude, I'm not tracking." Tyler looked carefully at his friend.

"And I'm betting the person who wrote this coded message based it on *Macbeth*. Miss Becky, have you got a copy around here somewhere? You'd need that to even try to decipher it."

"*Macbeth*? Sure. I've got a Shakespeare anthology in the bookcase."

"Perfect!" Alex continued, enjoying being the expert in the room. "If the quote is that easily recognized as something from *Macbeth*, then whoever wrote this was probably using that as a clue. You know, kind of signaling the right person that if you recognized the source, then you'd know where to look to solve the cryptogram."

He paused and smiled before adding, "Of course, that's *if* you know how to decipher a cryptogram . . . which I do."

Becky left to retrieve a copy of Shakespeare from her books while Alex slid Jamie's laptop over and in front of him. He began to type a search query based on the words "Hancock" and the date "1902."

"Something happened in 1902," Alex announced as he hit *enter*.

"Why do you say that?" Tyler asked.

"'Cause whoever made these extra notes on the map must have assumed the right person would recognize *Hancock 1902* and connect it to something that most people, or at least *one someone*, would know about back then."

"Makes sense," Jamie agreed, nodding her head. She walked over to make another cup of tea and give the kids some space around her laptop.

"Not looking too good." Mac peered over Alex's shoulder at the initial results coming up. He was scrolling through pages of search results pretty quickly. Clearly Alex knew how to do this kind of online research.

Tyler suddenly slapped Alex on the shoulder. "Hey, wait a minute! There's a *Fort Hancock*. Right? I saw an exit for the town of Fort Hancock on I-10 just before you turn off to go to Eric's ranch!"

"He's right," Mac agreed. "I see it every time we go out there."

"Perfect! Let's try it." He typed Fort Hancock and 1902 and pressed *enter*.

As Becky returned to the kitchen with her old college textbook *The Complete Works of William Shakespeare*, she found Jamie, Tyler, and Mac silently staring over Alex's shoulder.

"What did you find while I was gone?" she asked, curious to know what had made them all so quiet all of a sudden.

Alex looked up and slowly turned the laptop in Becky's direction so she could read the search result on the screen. It was a newspaper archive site showing an article published in the *El Paso Herald* on October 22, 1902.

Bandits Attack Ft Hancock Payroll Convoy: $6,000 Stolen!

Mac read the brief account aloud. It told of a bold daylight attack on a payroll wagon and its armed escorts just before it arrived at Fort Hancock on the afternoon of October 21. Two masked bandits had quickly removed four small strongboxes from the wagon as six armed riders were seen looking on from their covering positions above and alongside the Fort Hancock road.

The armed escorts had not fired a single shot following the surprise ambush. The reporter with the *Herald* said one of the guards told him they immediately recognized that they were surrounded and outgunned. That part struck Tyler as kind of odd. The bandits had disabled the wagon, stolen all but one horse, and were last seen escaping south toward the Rio Grande River. This had led to speculation by the reporter that the robbers had been "banditos," Mexican guerilla fighters, that were common in the area in 1902.

Becky broke the thoughtful silence. "$6,000 in 1902 would be worth a small fortune today! Especially if that payroll was transported as gold coins."

"Not sure what *s* means, but if that little pencil notation— Hancock '02—really does refer to the robbery," Jamie mused, "then maybe we really do have a treasure map!"

"Yes *and* no," Alex corrected. "It's a treasure map only *if* we can decipher the code and if it tells us where exactly to find the stolen payroll." He smiled and added, "And if it's still there." He picked up Becky's *Shakespeare*. "Let's see what we can do about solving this."

16

THE CODE IS CRACKED

ecky felt sorry for Ryan and Eric when they walked in that evening. Neither really knew what hit them. Eric had flown out to an oil field in the Permian Basin that morning to deliver some parts for a damaged drill rig. That afternoon he'd flown back—bringing two cash-paying passengers to El Paso. Because tonight was the new weekly family dinner night, Ryan had stopped by the airport to pick up Eric on the way home. Neither of them was sure just what to make of the story they heard as soon as they walked into the kitchen.

Jamie led off, explaining how the theft at the gallery had started the whole thing. She'd been telling everyone about the theft, then they figured out the stolen photo was of a place that Alex already knew about . . . then the name "Gunther" came up . . . and then she remembered the notebook and map they'd found at Eric's trailer . . . and then they noticed the strange notes and rhyme . . . and one thing just led to another.

Mac explained how Alex had figured out that the notes were part of a code based on *Macbeth* and that the map they'd found earlier was actually a claim map, but now they knew it was really a coded treasure map related to a robbery out near Fort Hancock in 1902.

Eric and Ryan looked quizzically at each other: what had they walked into . . . and what did any of this have to do with a stolen photograph from an art gallery? "So, let me get this straight," Ryan interrupted. "You found some kind of coded message based on *Macbeth* on the map?"

"Yes, but—well, it might be easier to show you how the code works first." Jamie turned to Alex. "Show Ryan and Eric how you figured it out." Alex opened the map on the kitchen island and pointed to a series of random letters arranged like words in a sentence but the "words" didn't make sense.

"That almost looks like some of the made-up words I had to memorize in the seventh grade." Ryan glanced over at Becky and winked. "We had to recite the 'Jabberwocky,' a poem by Lewis Carroll. It's full of impossible words that look like gibberish, just like these."

"Except you can pronounce the words in that poem," Becky laughed. "These letters are grouped like words but clearly they're not meant to be pronounced in any language."

"But since Miss Becky recognized this as a quote from *Macbeth*, I had an idea that maybe this was some kind of a code," Alex said confidently.

Ryan and Eric looked at the opening dialogue by the witches and then at the odd collection of letters masquerading as words:

Cdbgb akad cdbgb bogd labg nc0h ata0d vgz. Azda akad

azda uegd azeb axgd maj0b wld0c. cnl azeb miid atdc wlji ajec
vtr. Dcpbh atdc qoh atdc xcdc ajec bbtah.

"Sorry." Eric shook his head. "I'm not connecting."

"It's a book key cypher!" Mac interrupted, eager to show what they'd found out.

"What's a book key cypher?" Ryan felt like he was missing something obvious yet elusive.

Alex continued. "In a book key cryptogram a secret message is built on words found in a book. But to make it work, you've got to reference a copy of the same book the first person used and they need to have cleverly told you where to look to locate the right words in that book."

"And that book is . . .?" Ryan was still confused.

"In this case it's not a book, but a play," Becky explained. "The cypher's key uses the classic text of *Macbeth*, the play that William Shakespeare wrote right around the year 1606. There are thousands, maybe millions, of identical copies, and actors and scholars study it by numbered lines. Kind of like references to verses in the Bible."

"So," Tyler continued, "if I told you to go to Act 1, Scene 3 of the play and find the fifth word in line 11, you could find the exact word you need to replace one of the nonsense words in the coded sentence!" he announced triumphantly.

"Then how do you get that from these gibberish looking words?" Eric asked patiently. He was beginning to see where this might be going.

"That was the easy part," Alex grinned. "Whoever coded this message just used a really simple code: a letter-to-number cypher. To start to decode the message, you need to turn each letter into a number!"

"Show me." Ryan was starting to sense where this was headed as well.

Alex found an envelope in the stack of mail on the counter and turned it over. Down the length of the envelope he wrote all twenty-six letters of the alphabet in a column. Then in a second column, he wrote a number beside each letter—beginning with the number 1 beside A and finishing with 26 beside the letter Z. When he'd finished, he wrote the letters C-D-B-G-B below the chart and handed the pen to Ryan. "Okay, now use this key and give me the numbers for this first word in the message."

Ryan immediately understood the code. He quickly referenced Alex's list and began writing down numbers. When he'd finished, C-D-B-G-B had become 3-4-2-7-2.

Excited to show how to use what they had figured out, Becky opened her copy of *The Complete Works of William Shakespeare* and turned to *Macbeth*. While they watched, she showed Eric and Ryan how the first two numbers—3 and 4—became Act 3, Scene IV. She turned to Act 3 and found Scene IV then counted to line 27 in the manuscript. Finally she pointed to the second word. "So, the string 3-4-2-7-2 solves as the word *twenty*."

"Got it." Eric was impressed. "So if we just jump to the punch line, what exactly does all this mean?"

Alex pulled out a paper and read aloud the long hidden text:

Twenty and twenty steps west
left is best.
Ten and ten steps more
look under foot.
Seven steps down
a hole be found.
Remove a door
a storehouse be found.

Tyler added a clarification. "We've decided that since the

word *paces* isn't found in *Macbeth*, the person decoding the cypher is supposed to know each of those *steps* is actually a pace, which means about a yard."

"So 120 feet to a place where you can turn left, then another 60 feet to another place where you go down 20 or so feet to whatever it is you're going to find?" Eric summarized slowly to see if he was tracking.

"Pretty much," Alex replied. Everyone was silent for a minute as the meaning of the poorly written poem began to sink in. It certainly sounded like directions to find something. And that *something* seemed likely to be the cash stolen in the Fort Hancock robbery of 1902.

What made the most sense about it all was that this was written on a map that documented an abandoned silver mine that was only fifteen or twenty miles from where the robbery had occurred. So it really was possible that a treasure had stayed hidden all these years deep in some tunnel of the long abandoned Gunther-Morrison silver mine.

That left only one question if you knew exactly where that old mine was located and where to find the loot inside that mine . . . how could you possibly ignore the opportunity to see if the treasure was still there?

17

THEY CALL THIS ART?

The professor sat in the back corner of the coffee shop. He glanced at the canvas bag on the chair beside him, then carefully scanned the coffee shop to see if anyone was staring at him. The cheap reusable grocery bag was just the right size to hold the framed color photo he'd taken this morning from a local art gallery. But his furtive survey of the room wasn't because anyone here in the coffee shop would guess it was stolen. Mainly he was nervous. He'd never done anything like this before. He shook his head and realized that wasn't true. Two days ago he could have said he wasn't a thief. But now, well . . . Yesterday he'd stolen an expensive quadrunner from a trailer out in the desert and a pair of binoculars from that yellow trailer next door. Now this print. He was disappointed in himself.

Satisfied no one was paying any attention to him, he slowly pulled out the framed photo and set it on his lap. *How did they know? Who was this Jamie and why had she taken this perfect aerial photo of his silver mine? What was she up to? Why would she put his secret up on the wall of an art gallery for everyone to see?*

He studied the photo for the third time today and picked out the entry to the mine shaft. Of course, he finally admitted to himself, you'd have to know it was there. He looked more closely this time. You couldn't actually see any of the details of the mine entrance in the photo. *But still, what did she know about his mine?*

He took a sip of his coffee and glanced around again. It was strange having to hide out in coffee shops and bookstores. But he was determined to stay away from Tony the Fish or any of the people who were probably looking for him. Today was Friday. After pulling his Subaru free yesterday, using the winch on the four-wheeler he'd "borrowed," he'd driven back to El Paso. But he'd been careful not to drive straight to his house. He watched enough spy movies and detective shows to know better than that. *Not with a big-time loan shark probably out looking for him!*

He'd parked several houses down the street and carefully examined everything on the street. It took a few minutes but he finally noticed a red Nissan Xterra he hadn't seen on his street before. Even more ominous, a guy was just sitting in it. *Just sitting there!* No one ever just hung out in their car. Not on his street in the middle of the afternoon!

That was all he'd needed—it confirmed what he'd suspected. Tony the Fish was looking for him. He'd assigned one of his goons to stake out his house and wait for him to show up. But he was careful to stay calm. No need to panic—at least, not yet. He turned around in a nearby driveway and once safely back to the highway, he'd driven straight to a cheap motel out on I-10 and checked into a room.

Next had been the surprise at the art gallery later that evening. After showering and changing into his best pair of jeans, he'd gone for a drive and somehow ended up in the city arts district. He was just wandering around when he looked in a gallery and saw this photo taken by a new local photographer. Someone named Jamie Smythe.

He'd immediately recognized the subject. After all, he'd seen a satellite photo of his mine only a hundred times or more on Google Earth! Certainly enough to recognize that this carefully framed photo by "Jamie Smythe" showed his mine! He became obsessed. He *had* to get that picture, but at $650 he couldn't afford it. So he decided to steal it. That voice was telling him to be calm . . . act cool . . . casual . . . like any customer. But as he wandered around, his attention was not on the artworks but on spotting all of the security cameras and seeing if he could find the manager's keys.

There are times when busy managers in small shops carelessly leave their ring of keys near the register behind the front counter. This was one of them. When the manager stepped into the backroom to check on a print for another customer, it took only a moment for the professor to slip the front door key off the ring and into his pocket. Making a duplicate and returning the original an hour later was easy. Then at precisely 5:30 this morning he'd used it to let himself in. Ignoring the digital voice on the alarm reminding him that he had just sixty seconds to enter the alarm deactivation code, and avoiding the shop's video cameras, he'd walked quickly to the photo, tucked it under his arm and left, locking the door behind him—all the while avoiding the video cameras. He was around the corner and getting into his car when he heard the alarm go off.

Now no one would have access to Jamie Smythe's photo of his mine. The professor put it back in the bag and pulled out his phone. *Who was this Jamie and what exactly did she know about his silver mine?* He started searching social media sites for info about her. *That photo couldn't have been a coincidence!* A Facebook page for her artwork popped up along with a photo of her at the show's opening yesterday afternoon. She was smiling at the camera with her arm around the shoulder of a guy identified as her fiancé "Eric."

This Eric person looked familiar. He used his fingers to stretch and zoom in more closely. Suddenly he knew why Jamie's face on the gallery brochure looked so familiar to him! She and her fiancé were the same people he'd watched from the yellow mobile home yesterday morning. The quadrunner he'd stolen belonged to Eric.

As he looked at their faces, it suddenly occurred to him why he hadn't found his map and notebook in his backpack. He'd looked for them in all his bags when he got to his motel room, but hadn't found them. Then he remembered how angry he'd been with himself the other night at the trailer . . . so angry that he'd tossed the notebook and map at the sofa and missed. They'd fallen on the floor and he should have picked them up, but he'd been in a funk and gone straight to bed. Yesterday morning when he found the four-wheeler, he'd been so excited that he left in a rush. Totally forgot the notebook and map. *Dang!*

Of course, now the professor could just imagine Jamie Smythe and Eric the Fiancé and the kids finding them. Did they know where his silver mine was? *Why would you take this photo if you didn't?* After a moment he calmed himself and took another drink of coffee. Of course there couldn't be a connection between his notebook and the photo, not that quickly. But still, what if they followed the map to the mine? Well, they'd find a worthless abandoned silver mine just like he had . . . right?

This satisfied him for a moment. Then other thoughts

occurred to his fearful, suspicious mind. *What if they knew a geologist? Maybe they have more time to explore the mine than* he'd had. He'd run out of time to explore that last tunnel. *What if it hid an untapped, promising vein of ore? What if they found it before he did?*

He stood to leave. He still wasn't sure exactly what to do, at least not yet. He was convinced of one thing though. If the nosy photographer and her fiancé understood the map, they'd be going out to have a look at his mine. Probably this weekend. He was going to have to go back and make certain they didn't steal his claim!

18

A BREAK IN THE CASE

Special assignments were seldom as exciting as people think they are. That was Agent Harper's assessment of the plan for today. "I still can't believe you were able to persuade the boss to fund this kind of a stakeout, especially with Saturday overtime." He and his partner were sitting in a pickup truck watching the two-lane highway in front of them, waiting for a truck with horse trailers to go past.

Their stakeout was on the far side of an old gas station that looked like it had been abandoned in the 1960s. A decaying desert relic. They were on its north side and hidden from a car or truck approaching from the south. Even if they glanced back after they'd passed, the dust would make it hard to notice them. Spending the morning in the hot, windy cab of a pickup in West Texas wasn't Harper's first choice. Sitting in their air-conditioned office back in the El Paso Federal Building running data analysis would be much more comfortable.

"I've rarely gotten a bum tip from my man Fergie," Agent Ramirez finally replied. "He wouldn't have pinged me if it hadn't been such a crazy thing he had gotten wind of—Chris Gatto talking to someone on his phone about hiring some cowboys— with real horses and everything."

"I know he's good, but I hope Gatto wasn't just playing him to see if he was a snitch."

"You mean the old trick of setting up a possible informant with a story that is so unique only one person could have heard it and shared it?"

"Essentially, yes . . ." Harper paused when he heard a voice on the encrypted scanner radio: "Item One. Black Escalade. Dark tinted windows. No confirmation on occupants. Northbound. 11:08 a.m."

The voice on the scanner came back with a second report moments later: "Item Two. White F250. Two occupants. Pulling a triple axle horse trailer. Following item One. Northbound. 11:09 a.m."

"It sounds like your friend was spot-on after all." Harper grinned as he picked up his walkie-talkie and hailed their third partner who was inside the old station.

"Hey there, Skypants, got your ears on? Over."

"10-4, this is Skypants. Go ahead."

"Stand by for GO on the Hawk, over?"

"Copy that. Standing by for go on the Hawk."

Agent Ramirez turned his tablet back on and touched the app that would feed a video stream from the drone about to be launched. On a second app, which was floating over the corner of the video feed, he could see a map with a blue dot marking their location and a green dot for the drone hovering above them.

The noise of another vehicle in the relative silence of a windy desert carries a long way before the source arrives in sight—it was nice to have a two-mile heads-up that something was on its way. Moments later the black Cadillac Escalade passed, kicking up dust and bits of litter as it sped down the highway at a pretty fast clip. About thirty seconds behind it was a white heavy-duty pickup pulling a horse trailer, leaving its own wake of dust and debris as it raced past.

As soon as the tail wind of the trailer had passed, Agent Harper was on the walkie-talkie again: "Skypants, it's GO TIME. Copy?"

"10-4. Got it. Hawk is GO. Stand by for feed in 3 . . . 2 . . . 1 . . . She's up."

Immediately the camera on the drone provided an aerial view of their position as it continued its ascent and flew north along the highway, following the Escalade. Ramirez also watched the green dot of the drone tracing along the highway map in the other app. This latest feature, which had just been added to his software, let him anticipate where Chris Gatto and his hired cowboys might turn off as they made their way toward Rooster Canyon.

"Nice work, Skypants!" Agent Harper radioed to their drone operator. "We've got a good signal from Hawk. Over."

"10-4. All systems good. We're at 96 percent power and one mile downrange."

"Copy that, Skypants."

"If my guess is right, they're going to turn off just up here." Ramirez pointed to a road just a bit beyond the drone's green dot. On the real-time video monitor, he could see the turnoff coming up around a gentle bend as the Escalade started to slow down.

Harper got out his cell phone and rang David King, the

rancher who was waiting behind the old gas station in a second pickup truck with his brother and their gooseneck trailer carrying the four horses for today's stakeout. "You about ready to break the boredom and roll?" Harper asked in an empathetic voice. He was certain the two cowboys were as bored as he and Ramirez.

"Well, we're just playing solitaire on our phones," came the reply. "Was that who you're lookin' for—the boys that just went past?"

"Think so. The Escalade for sure and unless that pickup was just in a hurry to go ridin' they're probably the hired scouts for the day. We're gonna be ready to roll here in about two minutes."

"Not a deal, you've got us for the day," David replied. "By the way, that looked to be my son-in-law Eddie's F250. Looks like your guy has hired a very good scout. He's one of the best with these mountains."

"Small world." Harper shook his head.

"Naw, not really . . . just West Texas. Did you see two in the front cab?"

"Affirmative. Driver and a passenger."

"Well, then, the other is probably his buddy Roland."

Harper shook his head at the coincidence of the FBI hiring David King and his brother, Matt, to help them track Chris Gatto, who in turn had hired David's son-in-law and his best friend as *his* scout.

As soon as Ramirez confirmed that the Escalade and pickup had turned off to go up the canyon road, he gave Harper the green light to move out. Ramirez continued to watch the video feed, which showed the Escalade and horse trailer stopped on the side the road about a mile beyond the turnoff and Gatto and the two cowboys opening the horse trailer. "How are we on drone time?" he asked Harper.

"Skypants, how are we on fly time? Over."

"We've got 58 percent power, six miles downrange, systems fine. Need to execute return in four minutes at current range."

"Perfect. Come on out and jump in the truck so we can roll. You can reroute the drone's return to the truck's location."

As soon as their drone operator was back in the truck, Harper asked Ramirez the big question they'd avoided talking about before now: "How are you on riding a horse?"

"Sounds like a blast!" Ramirez grinned and continued watching Gatto and his cowboys as Harper shifted into gear and slowly began rolling across the gravel lot onto the old blacktop highway. David and his brother, Matt, followed. Soon they were closing the six-mile distance between them and their quarry.

Harper wanted to keep some distance and stay out of sight, but also be close enough to shorten the drone's fly-back path and keep it airborne longer. If everything timed just right, they'd be landing the first drone and launching a fresh one at the same time with little break in visual coverage.

Ramirez and Harper reviewed the important Rules of Engagement for the day: First, there was no crime—not yet. Two, this was a surveillance job for now. They intended to watch, document, and stay clear, to see exactly what it was that Gatto—AKA the Cat— had in mind. Something had to be going down to draw him up here to Rooster Canyon this afternoon. Whatever it was, there would be plenty of surveillance video in the archive from the drone.

Of course, they didn't have to state the obvious: Number three, if there was trouble—they were ready to handle whatever came up. After all, they were FBI.

19

ATVS IN THE DESERT

I t was just after lunch by the time Eric, Jamie, Tyler, Mac, and Uncle Ryan made it to the ranch. Tyler was excited that Mac's parents and Eric had agreed to the idea of checking out the treasure map. A little surprised, actually. He thought adults were supposed to say no to crazy ideas like a real-life treasure hunt. But here they were at Eric's ranch and ready to head up into the mountains out in the distance.

Ryan had been surprised at his own sudden rush of curiosity after the map was explained. He and Becky had debated whether they were totally crazy to endorse the search. In the end, they decided it would be a lifelong memory for everyone—even if it was a huge long shot. And it was the weekend and nothing was on the calendar anyway, so why not? He and Eric had discussed concerns about what condition they'd find the old mine shaft in and if it was too dangerous, they'd agreed to bail out and avoid taking risks that were over their heads.

Ryan and Eric secured their equipment onto the front racks of the three four-wheelers: two big coils—over 200 feet—of climbing rope, flashlights, LED headlamps, and Eric's belaying harness if they needed it for serious climbing. When everything was ready, Eric explained the travel plan. "Ryan, you and I will each ride one of the quads, and Mac, you can drive the third— so you'll stay with us." He winked at her and Mac grinned back. She knew it had been a toss-up whether she or Tyler got the third ATV. She was excited to have won this round!

"Jamie, you and Tyler will drive the Cruiser. As we make our way to Rooster Canyon, we'll see how far we can get the truck up the North Trail and park if we have to."

He turned to Mackenzie with a more serious look. "I know this all sounds like fun, Mac—but it's also potentially pretty dangerous, okay? So it's really important that you stay in between me and your dad— be careful out there today. Got it?"

"Yes sir," Mac nodded then grinned at her dad before adjusting the strap on her helmet to make certain it was on tight.

"No hotdogging, okay?" Her dad wanted to make certain Mac knew he was just as serious as Eric.

"Yes, sir," she repeated and turned to give Eric a thumbs-up that she was ready.

Jamie and Tyler climbed into the old Toyota FJ40. Tyler knew it had been developed to be one of the toughest, most reliable, 4WD trucks on the planet. Every day, they got people around in some of the most remote and rugged corners of the world—like the mountains of Pakistan, the jungles of Central America, the Alaskan wilderness, and the deserts of North Africa. This trek was the kind of expedition it had been designed for. He was excited to get to ride in it.

"Ready to roll?" Jamie leaned out the open driver's window and looked at Eric.

"Let's do it."

As the three quad runners headed out in single file, Jamie shifted the Toyota into gear and soon they were bouncing over a very faint track that led across the desert brush toward the range of mountains out beyond.

20

THE WAITING GAME

Ramirez and Harper had been sitting in the truck watching the video feed for almost an hour with the horses unloaded and standing by, ready to saddle at a moment's notice. They'd traded out drones every fifteen minutes to keep a freshly charged camera in the air, which gave Ramirez a continuous real-time video stream of Gatto and the cowboys. Unfortunately, this was the hurry-up-and-wait part of a surveillance operation.

The reason for the delay was obvious: Gatto didn't know how to ride a horse. He was clearly a city boy who'd never been near a horse, let alone ridden one! The longer they watched, the more comical the whole situation became. The first horse they saddled wouldn't cooperate. The second seemed spooked by Gatto's inability to get into—and *stay* in the saddle. After it successfully shed him three times, the cowboys brought out a mahogany-colored horse that was more patient. Shortly after the fourth drone trade out, Gatto had learned enough of the basics for them to head up the trail toward Rooster Canyon and the mountain ridge on its western and northwestern rim.

One thing that caught Ramirez's attention was a fourth horse, now saddled, trailing behind one of the cowboys on a lead. He raised an eyebrow and saw Harper nod. *Who was Gatto expecting to find and bring back on the extra horse?* With Gatto on the move, the agents headed back to the horse trailer to review their best tracking options. It'd be tricky in this terrain to follow but remain unseen. Could they watch by drone and still get to Gatto quickly enough if they had to?

After a quick discussion of pros and cons over a bottle of water, they agreed they could get to most anywhere in the canyon in roughly forty-five minutes if they had to, and decided to give Gatto and his scouts a head start and keep watching the video feed. After all, they'd have to come back this way regardless, so it wasn't like they could get away.

21

STEEP TRAILS AND VIEWS TO DIE FOR

The group of explorers created a rolling dust cloud from the ranch and across the desert, getting ever closer to the mountains. Soon they began the long climb up the rugged trail used by ranchers to cross from the west side. Finally the grade was so steep that Jamie had to stop and engage the Cruiser into four-wheel-high so she'd have more traction. Eric pulled up alongside and set the front locking hubs for her, then they moved out and continued the climb.

Jamie was showing off the skills Eric had taught her as the trail continued to deteriorate, particularly where large rocks that had tumbled down from the mountain cluttered the trail. Then at a switchback well up the trail, the left rear tire spun some gravel and the truck slid sideways. Tyler's heart raced as he gripped the door handle, hoping that the tire would catch and keep the Cruiser from sliding backwards and downwards in a slow loss of control.

He watched as Jamie quickly jerked the steering wheel to the right causing the tire to suddenly catch. She then immediately straightened the wheels and once more they began up the incline. Tyler noticed that the ATVs had all stopped on the switchback above to see if she could pull things out, and he was very impressed that Jamie knew exactly what to do.

They all finally made it through the switchbacks, but then the trail seemed to disappear. What lay in front of them was a rock-filled draw that almost went straight up. Eric got off his ATV and leaned on the door of the Cruiser to talk with Jamie. "You could drop it into four-low and give it a go . . . if you want."

There was a pause as Jamie leaned her head out the window, sizing up the challenge ahead. "Yeah, but I'm not so sure about that climb."

"Your call. We can leave the truck here and do the last couple of miles on the four-wheelers. No need to push it."

Jamie took one more look. "I suspect I could get about halfway up, but I'm just not sure about that top part. If we're going to have to leave the Cruiser anywhere, it might as well be here." She paused for a final look, then nodded her head. "Yup. I think this is where I leave it to the hard-core rock crawlers."

Eric smiled and nodded his agreement. It was a tough looking hill. He opened the door and held Jamie's hand while she climbed down from the truck. Tyler checked his map before getting out of the passenger seat. Alex had given them the GPS coordinates for the mine and he could see they were very close—like Eric said, probably within a couple of miles.

But until you were actually four-wheeling up a mountain trail it was hard to imagine just how challenging it was to navigate what looked like a short distance on a map.

Jamie raised the driver's side sun visor and tucked the keys under it before closing the door. "Just a little habit that means the keys are always with the truck if something happens," she told Tyler who was wondering why she didn't just stick them in her pocket. She climbed on the back of Mac's ATV and Tyler climbed up behind Ryan. Eric led off again, carefully negotiating the boulders in the middle of the draw as he worked his way up the hill. Then Mac and Ryan began snaking their way up the trail keeping a safe distance between them. At the top was a flat rock outcropping about twenty feet wide that stretched on beyond them for a mile or more. The mountain rose up to the left, and on their right, the flat, rocky ledge ended abruptly and fell away toward the canyon below.

Eric waited for Mac and Ryan to catch up. The view was spectacular but unnerving if you had any fear of heights. Jamie tried her best to take it in and ignore the drop-off. From the top of the draw, the old Cruiser looked impossibly far below them, and she was glad she'd decided to park where she did. The steep ascent wasn't impossible for the Cruiser, but she suspected even Eric would have found it challenging.

Eric glanced back down to see what Jamie was staring at. "Well," he offered, "I guess I might have gotten up that draw in the FJ40 . . ." Then he shook his head. "But I think leaving it down there was a good call." He smiled at Jamie and gave her a wink. "You'd really have to be patient to get up, around, and over those boulders!" Mac studied the lay of the draw herself for a moment, recalling some of the tips her uncle had taught her about four-wheeling and secretly imagined that she could get up it if *she* had the chance.

"Let's move on out." Eric shifted his ATV into gear and revved the engine as he started out. The other two quads followed in single file, and like Eric hugged the mountain side of the ledge.

Jamie glanced one more time to her right, at the steep drop-off. "These kind of heights give me a tingly sort of feeling in my gut." She yelled to be heard over the engines. "Kinda like butterflies . . . you know? I'm glad you're driving on this ridge and not me!"

"I know what you mean!" Mac said, glancing over toward the canyon. "At least the trail is nice and wide through here and we don't have to worry about getting too close to that crazy edge. Right?"

The trail continued to wind along as it traced the upper rim of the canyon wall. In the distance, it branched with the left fork trail taking them higher into the mountain while the right gradually led back down toward the canyon floor with several switchbacks along the way. One thing stood out: *the view from up here was amazing!*

Eric's voice crackled in the earpiece of Mac's helmet. "That fork up ahead is where this backside trail meets up with the main Rooster Canyon Trail. If you follow it to the right far enough, it comes out on Ranch-to-Market Road 504 down at the south end of the canyon. For what it's worth, RM504 eventually connects out south with I-10." He paused a moment then continued. "We'll take the left and head up higher to follow the coordinates Alex gave us."

Twenty minutes later, the three ATVs left the ridge and its dangerous drop-off and immediately began the steep and winding climb up the mountain. This part of the track was well maintained, just as Alex suggested it would be. Utility repair crews in heavy trucks used it to get to the microwave transmission towers on top. Better maintenance meant no big washouts to slow them down.

The well-kept trail was useful for a bit but soon they had to turn off onto a side trail and drop into one of the small valleys to find the Gunther-Morrison mine. They began a descent down a small niche in the fold between two ridges of the mountain. It was steep and rocky but not obstructed by any big boulders. At the bottom they negotiated a sharp turn that crossed another washout and slowed to a stop to decide exactly how to work their way across without getting stuck.

Once on the far side, the trail curved again and then ended abruptly at a wide clearing full of crushed rocks and the tailings from years of mining. Finally they could see what they'd come to find: heavy wooden timbers that held back the rocks which had tumbled down the mountain and framed the entrance to an old mine. But Mac's heart sunk. Boards were nailed across the opening and a pile of large rocks in front of the boards further guarded the entrance.

"Okay!" Jamie called out, "Everyone needs to hydrate before we get started!"

"Good call, Jamie!" Ryan caught Tyler's shoulder and wheeled him back toward the ATV to find their water.

"So, what's your plan, Eric?" They were all studying the imposing pile of rocks blocking the entry and Jamie was sitting on the side of her ATV beside him.

"I'm thinking Ryan, Tyler, and I should start moving those rocks while you and Mac unload all the equipment and get us ready for some exploring."

"Agreed." Jamie looked to Mac who nodded her head as well.

"Yeah," Mac added. "You boys go play in the rocks and we ladies will do all the unloading." She gave her uncle Eric a playful punch in the arm. "Don't forget your gloves!"

"And watch out for snakes," Jamie cautioned as the three picked their way over to the mine entrance. "Cause *they're* watching you!"

"On it." Eric paused to have a quick look around and then inspected each side of the rock he was about to climb over. *I hate snakes.*

22

IT'S NOT JUST THE SNAKES THAT ARE WATCHING . . .

I f Jamie and Mackenzie had looked above the ridge along the right side of the clearing—just up and to the left of the mine's entry—they'd have been startled. But they were so intent on unloading the equipment from the quad runners that they missed a frightening discovery. Someone was watching them. The notion of having to be cautious hadn't occurred to either of them. They hadn't even considered the possibility that someone else might be here.

After they'd finished, they rested against the ATV and watched the work underway. Everywhere you looked were rocks of every size. The guys had cleared enough of them that you could now see the rusty rails of a narrow gauge cart track coming from the mine and disappearing again under other debris in the clearing.

To the right of the entrance towered the mountain wall. Not a sheer vertical face like a rock quarry, but a rugged, steep climb interrupted by a series of draws created by ancient folds in the rock structure. You could probably climb it with some difficulty—and just hope that the boulders didn't come loose and go crashing down the mountainside.

Mac scanned the mountain and saw there'd been a lot of rock slides over the years. What she didn't spot was a navy ball cap, only slightly visible among the shadows and the gray and white of all those rocks above the entrance. It belonged to a man in a gray sweat-soaked tee shirt crouching behind a boulder. The professor anxiously watched the group that had invaded his mine site. He was outraged that his worst fears were true: That *Jamie person* . . . the one who took a picture of his mine and put it in her show at the art gallery . . . well, she really did know where the mine was, because here she was! And worst of all, she'd brought those kids, and another guy, and her fiancé—what was his name? Eric. Yes, that was it—Eric.

He took a swig of water from his bottle and carefully got out the binoculars he had stolen from the yellow trailer. *This is getting too complicated. What, exactly, are these people up to? They don't look like geologists. Unless maybe that guy they brought along is a geologist? There's no question they found Grandpa Gunther's notebook and map! What exactly is it they think they're going to do down there in my mine?*

All he could do now was watch and wait. He could see they'd brought ropes and a couple of small shovels, but nothing big. Then his brain came up with a sinister suggestion. *Maybe— maybe, after they get the boards off and go in . . . maybe I can get down there and nail the boards back on and trap them!*

He stopped himself and shook his head. The thought alarmed him. What was he thinking? Something serious could happen to them. No, he couldn't do that! He was just going to have to be patient and see what they were up to before he decided how he needed to protect *his* mine.

But something is up down there.

23

A VERY DARK PLACE

With powerful, LED headlamp bands on their heads, everyone was anxious to see what was inside. "Hey, Eric, did you notice how easily those boards pried off?" Ryan asked quietly.

"The nails looked new to me. Certainly not a hundred years old. Old ones are flat-squared and *very* rusty."

"Totally," Ryan agreed.

"Are we all set?" Tyler hadn't heard their exchange but was anxious to get inside.

"Think so," Eric replied. "Remember, we're going to stay in pairs. I'll take point, and Mackenzie, you stay with your dad. Tyler, you stick with Jamie and bring up the rear. Everybody good?"

There were nods all around. Jamie passed a coil of yellow

nylon rope to Ryan. "Our best estimate of forty paces would be about 120 feet," she said. "We'll use the coil of nylon rope as a measure. When you get to the rabbit ear and knot, you should be near the left turn we're looking for." She tied a loop at the rope's tail, and pulled it tight around a nail sticking out of the heavy timbers at the entry. She handed the coil to Mac who passed it to her dad.

"Okay, let's do it!" Eric ducked his head and began walking down the narrow tunnel. Ryan followed, spooling out the yellow line behind him and scanning the sides and the roof with his light.

Following close behind her dad, Mackenzie was looking down and watching where she stepped. She was curious about the old iron rails they were walking between. She guessed they were for the ore carts that were used when the mine was active. The tunnel was very narrow, so they were walking single file. If she didn't keep an eye on her feet, she was certain she'd trip and maybe twist her ankle. That would not be good! It surprised her how total the darkness was. So strange to be able to see only what your headlamp was pointed at.

Behind Jamie, Tyler was taking in all the excitement. He'd never even been in a cave before today, much less a mine, so this was all so incredible! His headlamp illuminated the ceiling as he looked up. It wasn't very high—it just barely cleared the top of his head. Every three or four feet there were rough-sawn timbers holding up roof boards to prevent a cave-in. He was glad he was wearing his skateboard helmet! The air smelled very stale—like old wood. But the other sensation that hit Tyler was the cool air. Outside it was about 100 degrees and they'd been hot and sweaty. But now, even though they'd only just started in, he could tell it was going to be cold and his sweat-soaked tee made it feel even colder.

"Everybody okay back there?" Eric called out from the front of the line. The muffled sound of his voice in the tunnel seemed kind of spooky to Mac. The walls were so narrow that anyone with claustrophobia would probably freak out. No way her friend Shaniyah could handle this tiny space.

"We're fine," Jamie shouted from behind Mac, and her voice also sounded strange as it echoed along the walls of the narrow passage. When they'd first started in, there was a shaft of light from the entrance that was sort of the opposite of a shadow. Looking back now, it was just a small dot behind them.

"Are you scared?" Mac asked Jamie quietly, looking back over her shoulder.

"Well, I didn't think the small space would bother me, but I think it does, kind of."

"You mean like claustrophobia?"

"Maybe a little," Jamie hesitated. "Not overwhelming or anything, but I sure wouldn't want to do this every day."

"I can't imagine what it must have been like to be a miner working every day in a tunnel like this," Mac whispered. She kept her hand lightly on her dad's shoulder as she walked behind him. Jamie had her hand on Mac's shoulder, and she assumed that since Tyler was bringing up the rear, he must be close behind Jamie.

"Hey, Mac!" Mac turned her head and the light from her headlamp swung along the wall and straight into Jamie's eyes.

"Yowzers!" Jamie lifted her hand from Mac's shoulder to shield her eyes from the bright beam.

"Sorry!" Mac looked away, but then accidentally blinded her again when she instinctively looked back to see if Jamie was okay. "Oops! Sorry again!" This time she didn't look back. "What do you want, Tyler?" she hissed, frustrated at herself.

"Can you see anything up ahead of Eric?" Tyler asked. "Is

there just the one tunnel or more coming up?"

Mac peeked up and over her dad's shoulders as far ahead as she could but was having a hard time anticipating where Eric was going to look next. It was pretty disorienting to look at anything other than what was just in front of her. "Can't tell." This time she kept her light on the wall as she turned to answer him.

"I think I see a shadow up ahead to the right, just about three more timbers beyond me," Mac's dad said quietly over his shoulder.

Mac made note of how odd it was that she and everyone else felt like they needed to talk so quietly in the tunnel.

Eric paused and turned around to make sure everyone was still there. "The tunnel has been curving a little to the right as we've been going deeper. Tyler, there's a small opening here on my right. Can you check your compass and tell me what direction this new tunnel points toward?"

Tyler opened the top of his brass compass box, illuminating it with his headlamp. He rotated the compass until the red diamond of the needle pointed to the N on the dial—the N was more to his left than the direction they were headed now. "Looks like that tunnel goes off kind of east," he said. "If we were in your plane, I'd tell you it was sitting at about 110 degrees."

"That helps! So basically east-southeast. Can't be the tunnel we're looking for."

"Are we already to the 120 foot knot?" Jamie asked Ryan.

"No, still quite a way to go."

"That's fine," Eric said. "Just wanted to check since the tunnel is about to curve sharply to the left and I can't see another passage yet."

The group started moving forward again. As each of them passed the side tunnel they turned to peer into it. Their headlamps penetrated only twenty feet or so before the darkness swallowed their light. But even what they could see in a glance was a large room that had been dug pretty deep. And the floor of the side tunnel wasn't rock and rail tracks—it was old wooden planks, which looked very precarious to Tyler.

Soon the narrow tunnel began to curve sharply to the left, and Tyler could no longer see any of the passageway behind them and ahead, only Jamie and a bit of Mac's right shoulder. Eric and Ryan were already out of sight around the bend. The curve continued for what seemed like a long time before it straightened out.

Ryan aimed his lamp at the rope. "Hey, Eric! I'm almost at the knot."

"Okay. I'm still not seeing another passage, but the tunnel is about to make a slight curve again. Maybe it will be around that bend."

Jamie looked over Mac's shoulder and trained her headlamp on the rope trailing from Ryan's hand. "Once you get to the 120 foot knot, there should be a zip strip marking every ten feet after that."

"Got it. Thanks, Jamie."

Everyone was quiet as they continued to step carefully on the tunnel floor. Whenever she looked down, Mac could see the rusted iron rails that the small ore cars would have run along to bring the raw silver out when the mine was active. About the size of small wheelbarrows, they would have been pushed up the tunnel by hand.

"You still okay, Jamie?" Mac asked.

"So far, so good. But, to be honest, I'm beginning to wish I'd stayed out with the ATVs."

"Try a drink of water," Mac suggested.

"Good idea." Jamie flipped open the lid of her water bottle and took a drink. "Much better," she sighed.

To Mac, it seemed like it had been twenty minutes since her dad had said they were passing the 120-foot mark and she was checking her watch when her dad suddenly stopped and she almost ran into him. "What's up?"

"I think I've found our tunnel." Eric announced and turned to check once more that everyone was still with him.

24

A CLOSER LOOK

Mac could see that the tunnel they'd been following continued ahead of them. Her light just barely illuminated a point where it seemed to curve to the right maybe twenty feet beyond where they'd stopped. But here, the tunnel had become almost twice as wide and the rail tracks split in a Y connecting to a second set of tracks that headed left into a new tunnel.

Eric swept his beam into the tunnel that seemed to match the instructions in the coded message. "Ryan, how about you step into this passage with me and hold up the light. Mac, Jamie, and Tyler can stay here in the main tunnel for now."

Tyler crowded alongside Jamie and Mac to have a look. From what he could see in the light of Ryan's work lamp, the tunnel quickly became a larger, extensively excavated side room. The rail tracks had been laid out along a rock ledge running the length of the room.

Mac's eyes followed the beam of Eric's headlamp to the remains of a pretty extensive network of platforms of wooden scaffolding and ladders along the walls. After the vein of silver ore had been exposed by blasts of dynamite, the miners had used them to dig into it with shovels and pickaxes.

Eric asked Ryan for what was left of coil of yellow rope. "I'm going to walk down this ledge for six zip ties. That should be sixty feet or about twenty paces. Let's see where that puts us." As the sixth marker played out, Eric stopped—and so did the rail tracks even though the ledge continued on for another ten or fifteen feet. A large stack of big rocks had been piled up as a barrier to prevent an ore cart from rolling off this end of the spur.

He carefully looked over the edge and figured the floor of the pit was probably forty feet or more below. But it wasn't a sheer drop. Ledges had been cut into the wall like stair steps every twelve to fifteen feet. A lot of engineering know-how had gone into extracting the ore from under this mountain.

"Tyler!" Eric called out. "Can you come over here with the climbing gear?"

Mac and Jamie stepped out of the way as Tyler squeezed past and carefully walked the length of the narrow rock ledge to Eric. Only after he got there did, he look over the edge. "Whoa! That's a long way down!"

"This will be tricky, so you need to be very aware of where you are at all times, okay?"

"Got it."

"Ryan? I need you over here, too."

After discussing Eric's plan, they began pulling gear from the equipment bag. Soon they'd secured a head rope and carabiner to the old mine track as well as a second carabiner and its belay rope as a safety line. When they were in place, Eric stepped into a climbing harness and cinched the straps snuggly around his waist and thighs.

"So here's the plan. I'm going to rappel down to the next ledge and see if I can spot that 'door' or whatever the clue might have meant. Tyler, you remember how we practiced belaying, right?"

"You control your rope for the descent and climb," Tyler confirmed. "We're just your backup. We'll play out your rope or pull up the slack as you need us."

"Unless you start falling," Ryan added. "In which case we're your brake."

"That's it!" Eric grinned.

After Ryan and Tyler moved back to create some working length in the safety line, Eric tossed the tail of his rope over the edge and listened for it to hit the floor. Then he stepped across the rope and threaded it through his harness, tightened his gloves, and gave a thumbs-up. After grabbing the rope both under his leg with one hand and next to his chest with the other, he backed over the edge, pushed away from the side, and let himself fall about five feet before swinging back into the wall with his feet bracing the impact. From there he began a slow walk down the wall by releasing small lengths of rope while searching the rock face for something resembling a door.

"See anything?" Jamie called out

"Nothing yet. The next ledge looks pretty safe, so I'm going to drop down a bit more so I can get my big flashlight out for a better look."

Ryan and Tyler played out a bit more rope as Eric descended. "Okay, hold it tight there. No slack!" Tyler and Ryan tightened their grip as instructed.

Eric slowly inched along the skinny lower ledge some twelve feet below, moving his flashlight along the wall, looking for a hole large enough for the kind of strong box used to transport gold and silver coins in the early 1900s.

The others kept quiet, not wanting to bug him while he searched in the dark space below. After what seemed like forever, Eric turned off his flashlight and clipped it to his belt. He'd looked over the entire face of the wall three times and found nothing. Maybe, he thought, they'd misunderstood the clue.

"Sorry, guys, there's nothing down here," he announced, clearly disappointed.

25

THE PROFESSOR GOES IN

Waiting is never easy. And waiting on the outside when you know something is going on inside is even harder if you have to guess what might be happening. The longer *those people* were down in *his* mine, the more curious and paranoid the professor became. Finally he decided to look. Carefully climbing down the rocks from the ledge where he'd been hiding, he made his way to the entrance of the mine.

But what to do next? For a while he paced back and forth, ducking his head into the doorway each time for a look, a listen. *Should I go in after them? But what if they see or hear me? There are five of them and only one of me.* Maybe his first thought was best . . . *cover up the entry and trap them. Leave them. No one would know.* But that wasn't going to happen. He'd become a thief, yes, but he was not going to do something that horrible.

He'd spent two weeks in the mine and its layout was like a map in his head. *He didn't need a light. He could creep in and find out what was happening. Yes! That was it!* He'd go in far enough to hear what exactly it was they were doing. After all, there were only five rooms and three tunnels—and he knew them all. He could easily get to a different tunnel or a room if they got too close. It would be so easy. *They'd never know I was there . . . beside them in the dark!*

The yellow rope caught his attention as he paced across the door once more. He remembered overhearing them saying something about "120 feet." That was it. He was going in.

He untied their rope from the timber post. He'd coil the rope as he went and leave it in a different passage. Yes! That would confuse them. When they tried to leave they'd get lost. They might have to try every tunnel to eventually find their way out. It made sense to him. Maybe they'd get so lost that once they finally made it out—well, *maybe they'd just leave and never come back!*

He went over the layout of the mine in his head. About 120 feet was the same as sixty of his steps. He tried to remember what was special about that distance. He knew the tunnel split off to the left about that far in. Then what? The main tunnel continued on, curved to the right, and ended in two large rooms and before that, there was that first room to the left. So maybe they were headed to one of those three rooms?

He stepped carefully so he didn't make too much noise, coiling the rope as he went. He didn't dare use his flashlight, so he counted his steps in his head. *Thirty-six . . . thirty-seven . . . thirty-eight . . . almost to the first room—the one on the right.* He kept his hand on the wall, expecting to discover the opening any moment.

Thirty-nine . . . forty . . . forty-one . . . Where was it? Forty-two . . . forty-three . . . he could hear muffled voices reverberating from the passages far ahead of him. But it was almost impossible to make out what they were saying. He was starting to worry that maybe he'd miscounted his steps or gotten himself mixed up. Where was that side turn? Forty-four . . . forty-five . . . His hands came to another of the timbers that held up the roof and as he reached his hand beyond it there was no wall . . . he'd found what he was looking for!

The first ore mined in the early days had come from this room. This would be a perfect way to confuse them! He tossed the coil of rope over the edge of the plank flooring he was standing on and listened for it to hit the floor. Then he remembered that this room had the oldest scaffolding anywhere in the mine. It had seemed unstable when he first explored so he didn't trust walking too far out.

Convinced that leaving the rope here would create the confusion he hoped for, he stepped back into the main tunnel. He was ready to follow the voices now, deeper into the mine.

26

CLOSING IN WITH THE COWBOYS

Agent Ramirez scanned a large topo map of the canyon spread out across the tailgate of the pickup truck that served as their command center. He and his drone wrangler, Hassan, tracked Chris Gatto by video as he and his two hired cowboys made their way up the rough trail along the south rim of Rooster Canyon. A red pencil line on the map tracked their progress.

Hassan pointed to where the South Trail ended at the peak of the mountain on the far side of the canyon. At the top stood a pair of cross-country microwave towers and accessing them was the primary purpose of this trail. He also pointed out a fork on the map where the North Trail branched off. He described it as a rough, four-wheel track that led down the far side of the mountain.

Meanwhile, Agent Harper was leaning against the side of the pickup chatting with David and his brother Matt. He was telling them how he'd ridden horses at his uncle's ranch when he was growing up, but it had been years since he'd been on another one.

David assured him it would feel like he'd just ridden last week once he climbed up into the saddle again.

Everyone was ready to ride, the four horses were saddled and standing patiently in the slight shade of the horse trailer, but it seemed like it was all hurry up and wait. Harper stepped around to check in with Ramirez and Hassan. They still weren't clear about what Gatto was up to.

The intel from the Fischer wiretap and their informant had been inconclusive. It had given them the heads-up about Gatto planning to work with some cowboys, but the lead about silver mines had been a dead end. There were no active silver mines in this part of West Texas. They guessed the professor that Gatto and Tony had discussed might be the geologist named Dr. Jasper Gunther. He'd been reported missing eight days ago by his office assistant, but there was no evidence of foul play. Although the FBI had been watching his house, they hadn't spotted anyone coming or going. Their best guess for now, and the basis for today's surveillance, was that it had something to do with Tony's drug business. That seemed like the only reasonable explanation for why an urban crime boss would have his enforcer out in this wilderness on horseback with rented cowboys.

Maybe Gatto was scouting a new drop zone for importing drugs. Or maybe Tony was about to get into something altogether new. Whatever was about to happen, it seemed pretty clear that Gatto was anxious to wrap up something crucial for his boss out here today.

They watched the monitor on the iPad showing Gatto's progress. He and the cowboys were still about two miles from the fork. Were they going up to the microwave tower or down the other side of the canyon?

Harper hated this waiting game—the boring part of investigative work. "I've got an idea," he finally said. "Let's get you up in a saddle and see what you think of riding. We may need to get underway soon . . . I want to be sure we're ready to ride."

"Might as well," Ramirez agreed.

27

LET'S TRY THIS AGAIN

"How far down are you?" Mac called out. She wasn't going to give up on the treasure hunt, at least not yet.

"Probably twelve feet," Eric answered, wondering what Mac was up to.

"Is there another ledge below you?"

"Yeah. Probably another ten or fifteen feet down. Why?"

"Do you think the directions might have assumed the next ledge, further down?"

"The clue was kind of vague. There is another ledge, so let me check that out."

Mac turned to Jamie. "Can I see your big flashlight?"

"Sure." She unclipped the light and handed it to Mac who flipped it on and trained it down along the wall, tracing the ledge below Eric. He looked away to shield his eyes from the powerful beam directed at him. "Sorry!" Mac hollered, then slowly worked the beam along the side of the wall that Eric had repelled down. It was a rough, but essentially flat vertical surface with no crevices, no "doors," or anything that was out of the ordinary. She swept the light on beyond, toward the far wall of the room.

That's when she noticed a gap in the ledge where part of it had sheared off. And beyond that, almost to the far wall, something caught her light. "What's that, Eric?" She kept her beam trained on what looked to her like a piece of old discarded mining equipment lying upside down on what remained of the ledge.

Eric pulled out his flashlight. "Looks like an overturned ore cart. Must've gone off the end of these rails and crashed down here."

"Is there any way you can get to it safely?" Jamie was tracking with Mac that it would be the perfect place to hide something because it was very difficult to get to.

Eric shined his light on the old wooden planking scattered on the floor of the pit below him. "Might be able to use one of those loose boards." Eric worked with Ryan and Tyler to rappel deeper and finally tied a rope on two long heavy planks that had probably been used for catwalks on the scaffolding over a hundred years ago. With tremendous effort, Ryan and Tyler hoisted them up to the second ledge while Eric used one of the old ladders to climb back up the wall. Then he pushed the pair of boards across the gap until they rested on the far side. They were thick, and the dry air in the mine had prevented them from rotting. If they were as strong as they looked, he could easily reach the ore cart. He carefully put one foot on it and then his full weight. They held!

Mac kept her light focused on the far side of the ledge as Eric put his back and the palms of his hands on the rock wall behind him . . . and inched sideways along the planks. The wood bowed slightly under his weight as he approached the middle but it was thick and strong and still held. Reaching the cart turned out to be the easy part, however. Getting it upright was going to be harder than anyone expected. It was so heavy that Eric couldn't budge it at all.

"What if we tie a rope to it and we pull from up here?" Ryan figured he and Tyler might be able to pull it over from where they were. Eric agreed it might work, so they tossed down an extra rope. He tied it to the axle of the cart's wheels since it was upside down, and tugged on it to make sure the knot was going to hold, and gave Ryan and Tyler a thumbs-up.

"I'm going to watch from the other side of the plank while you pull if you don't mind," Eric said with mock sarcasm before he inched his way back across the board. "And don't forget, let go of the rope *fast* if the cart decides to take a plunge after you tip it over. Don't want it to drag you two off the ledge, okay?"

"Good call!" Ryan acknowledged before tightening his grip on the rope.

He and Tyler and grunted and pulled; the cart was heavy and stubborn. Finally, though, they got it rocking, and all at once, it reached its tipping point and rolled over. But as it landed upright, its back wheels missed the ledge and with a loud screech of bending metal and the crack of splitting wood, the cart slid off the edge and plunged into the darkness below, taking the rope with it to the bottom of the pit.

"Eric was right," Tyler said simply as he tried to regain his composure at how suddenly the cart had flipped and gotten away from them. All beams of light were now focused on where they had last seen Eric.

"Are you okay?" Jamie shouted over the echo and reverberation of the cart's crash.

"I'm fine." Eric aimed his high-powered light at where the cart had been just moments ago. "And," he added after a brief pause, "I think we are *all* going to be fine when you get a look at what I'm looking at." Mac moved her flashlight to the same place as Eric's, and she and Jamie gasped as they realized what they were seeing.

The story of the 1902 Fort Hancock Robbery was going to get its first new chapter in over 115 years!

28

BOXES

The curve ahead looked familiar. The professor recalled that the tunnel to the right led to a single large excavation—the biggest of the five rooms—and the one to his left led to three rooms. The first two were large; the third was where the miners had apparently lost the ore vein and abandoned their work.

As he crept around the curve, the voices became louder and more distinct. But suddenly there'd been an awful, incredible crash and everything became silent. He slowly peered around the curve. Light spilled into the tunnel from the room but he didn't see anyone. They all must be inside, he realized. They didn't sound close, so he cautiously approached the entry and saw them on the far end of the ledge looking down at something. Caution returned and the professor stepped back into the darkness. He needed to know what was going on, but not be seen.

"Okay," said one of the men, "toss the rope down." The voice came from below the rest of them, and the professor assumed he must be on one of the lower ledges. *Ropes,* he thought. That was the challenge of exploring an old mine. You had to do so much climbing and rappelling with ropes. He listened and waited and a few minutes later the voice called up again from below: "Okay, the rope's secure! Go ahead and pull the last box up."

Box? The professor had spent many hours in the mine and had never found any boxes except for empty wooden dynamite crates. *What kind of a box?* Then as the boy and the man who wasn't Eric-the-fiancé pulled up the rope, the professor spotted what looked like an early 1900s-era trunk, kind of like the ones pioneers used when they moved West in the old days. This box was smaller than those, but it seemed to be heavy . . . it took a lot of effort for them to raise it to the ledge.

The longer he stared, the more confused he felt. It looked like a pirate's treasure chest. Then he spotted a second box just like it . . . and then a third, *and* a fourth! *Four boxes?* And then, to his horror, he heard the crunch of gravel under his shoe.

"What was that?" The light on the girl's headband swept the wall, coming his way. He pulled his head out of the doorway just as it beamed into the tunnel. He almost panicked when he saw a faint outline of himself on the wall across from him. But before the shape could register with anyone, the light disappeared.

"Probably just a loose rock," the boy said as his headlamp similarly swept the doorway. But this time, the professor was further back so there was no shadow on the far wall. The group began discussing how they were going to get the boxes out and seemed surprised at how heavy they were.

What would make them so heavy? He cautiously peeked

around the corner of the doorway again. They were trying to decide whether or not to open them. Jamie's fiancé decided the dad could carry the front of the first box, the boy could carry the back of the second box, and he'd get in between and carry a handle of both. Jamie and the girl could lead them out, then they'd come back for the other two.

He thought quickly—when everyone was getting their things together they'd make enough noise to not notice the sound of his footsteps. He decided to slip across the entry and hide in the darkness of the tunnel beyond the spur and then follow them as they left. First out was that Jamie-photographer person, then the girl carrying a heavy backpack, their headlamps flickering and dancing on the walls and ceiling as they looked around. Last came the man-box-man caravan. They all paused until Jamie finally spotted the yellow nylon rope they'd left as their guideline. She fed it through her hands as she led the group back down the passageway the way they had come.

This was going to be interesting, he thought: the string of them following their guide rope into that side room. They'll be confused and have to turn around with those two heavy boxes and go back to look for a turn they'd missed. He smiled at the thought of his plan unfolding.

The lights of the group's headlamps filled the curve in the passage and gradually dimmed, leaving the professor in total darkness and his thoughts quickly returned to the boxes. *How can I get a look at what's in them? What's so important and how did they know to come looking for them? But now that they've found them—well, they're my boxes, yes?* He nodded to himself. *Of course they are. Because this is my mine.*

Well, sort of, he corrected, allowing that it probably had belonged to his grandpa Gunther. *Although there is that pesky Morrison name. But it's been over a hundred years, and the mine*

153

has long since been abandoned. And I found the map! He'd long ago decided this was his mine, which meant whatever was in those boxes had to be *his,* too.

Of course!

29

SIMPLY FOLLOW THE YELLOW ROPE

Jamie was going to be very glad to get out of here—the clammy air and complete darkness were really starting to freak her out. Her anxiety had been less intense when they were in the room where they'd found the boxes, but now she was in the lead and it was like the darkness ate the beam of her headlamp. The black never ended and she was becoming increasingly panicky

She continued to follow the rope, grasping it hand-over-hand. It hadn't been so difficult on the way in when she'd been behind Mac and Ryan and Eric with Tyler behind her. But now there was only her lamp to illuminate the void ahead. Mac's light helped some, and her hand on Jamie's shoulder reassured her she wasn't alone. But one moment it was comforting, and the next it seemed to weigh a ton. It was a nagging reminder that with every step, everyone was depending on her to get them out. She tried to breathe deeply but it didn't help. It couldn't be too far now. It was just at the end of this rope.

And . . . yet . . . it was so dark—plus, the tunnel seemed to be getting narrower. Fear crushed her lungs and she began to breathe even harder with every step. It didn't help that they had to walk slightly hunched over because of the low ceiling. Funny that she hadn't noticed the downhill incline on the way in, but now it was very clear that they were trudging uphill, which made things worse.

Behind her, the guys struggled with the weight of the boxes. Eric said he reckoned they were at least ninety pounds each. Since he handled freight on his plane for a living, she was pretty sure his guess was spot-on. Now, if the old rope handles will just hold up—they were thick but looked like they might be brittle after a hundred years.

"You okay, Jamie?" Mac asked once more. It was almost as if she could sense her discomfort.

"No. Not really," she admitted, whispering cautiously.

"Claustrophobia again?"

"Pretty much," Jamie looked over her shoulder, keeping her light pointed to the ceiling, and checked on everyone.

"We're all still here!" Tyler called. He felt like he needed to catch his breath before he could say anything else. His share of this box was super-heavy!

"Hey, Eric?" he asked when he could speak again. "How about we stop for a sec so I can adjust my hold on this strap."

"Jamie, we need to stop a second," Eric called ahead.

Although she didn't want to spend a second more in the mine than she had to, she knew she had to get a handle on her anxiety. "Okay, but make it quick. I'm getting kinda anxious to see blue sky again."

Then, as they set the boxes down, Tyler thought he heard something behind him. He glanced over his shoulder but saw nothing, just the shadows of the timbers that lined the tunnel slowly curving away behind them. He stretched his back, rubbed his hand, and reached down to pick the box up again. "Okay, we can keep going." But as they began to move, Tyler once more thought he heard something and turned to look.

"What's going on, Tyler?" Eric asked.

"Probably nothing," he said, not convincing himself. "Just thought I heard something behind me."

"Yeah, you probably did, like a rat or some other critter. I'm surprised we haven't seen anything skittering around before now."

Tyler was definitely creeped out at the thought of a rat right behind him. "Yeesh!"

Up ahead, Jamie was getting into the hand-over-hand rhythm of following the yellow rope and starting to pick up her pace. She was focused on their exit: She could imagine the blue sky, fresh air, and bright sunlight on her face. She'd finally be able to breathe deeply! At that very moment she felt the ground under her foot change from rock to something hollow-sounding and bouncy like wood. But before she could react, she'd taken a second step and a third. Suddenly there was a snapping sound like a board cracking and from below came the groans of splitting wood and the shriek of nails being pulled from ancient boards.

Just as she realized she wasn't on solid ground, her feet were sliding out from under her and she was suddenly on her bottom, sliding down a plank in slow motion, plunging into the darkness. As her headlamp cast strange and frightening shadows on the walls around her she screamed and turned her head, searching for Mac. But instead of finding Mac she felt an explosion of pain as the noise stopped and suddenly everything was incredibly silent and still.

The last thing she remembered before passing out was a horrible, throbbing pain shooting up her leg—*like it was on fire!*

30

THE FLOOR IS MISSING AND SO IS JAMIE

In the noise and confusion Mac had also started to fall, but when she'd grabbed at the air, her hand found the edge of the scaffold. Now she found herself hanging from a board with her feet dangling in the darkness. Dropping his end of the box, Ryan fell to his knees, and grabbed his daughter under one arm as Eric lunged forward to grab the other. Together the two of them pulled Mac off the broken plank and into the tunnel, away from the edge of the dark pit.

"Are you okay?" Ryan pulled Mackenzie to him in a hug that almost crushed her.

She was crying—more from fear and adrenalin than from anything hurting. She looked at her dad through her tears and mumbled and nodded yes. Then she looked back over her shoulder toward the dark space that Jamie had fallen into and began to cry again. In the light of their headlamps they could see that below them—maybe twenty or more feet down, Jamie lay motionless on a pile of broken wood and fallen scaffolding. Mac screamed when she realized what she was seeing.

"Ryan, take Mac on out and make sure she's okay!" Eric surveyed the scene below, then called after them, "Get back soon, though, I'm gonna need your help." As Ryan headed toward the entrance with Mac, Eric pulled out his flashlight for a better look below where Jamie lay unconscious.

"Is she dead?" Tyler was trying to hold back tears, afraid of what he'd seen.

Eric shook his head. "I don't know, Tyler. I gotta get down there fast. Help me with the bag." Together they hurried to get the ropes and harness out of the equipment bag. Tyler used a small hand pick to dig gravel and rock out from under the base of the rail track while Eric quickly maneuvered into his harness. Tyler then secured a head rope and a carabiner around the track and clipped the lead rope to it while Eric waited in the shallow entry to the collapsed scaffolding. When everything was cinched tight, he tossed the end of his rope into the pit below and began to thread both it and the belay rope through his harness.

As Eric was pulling his rope to check it was tight, Tyler suddenly noticed something odd in the light of Eric's headlamp—something that didn't make sense—the yellow rope. He glanced to his right toward the entrance and was puzzled by what he didn't see: yellow rope. He peered beyond Eric to examine the debris below. *How could all the rope be in the pit with Jamie? Even if she pulled some down when she fell, the rest should still be attached back at the entrance of the mine.*

"Eric, look at the guide rope. Why's it all down there in the pit? One end used to be tied to a post back at the entrance. I watched Jamie do it."

Eric looked back down the tunnel as far as his light would allow and saw the rope they'd been following trailing back. But when he searched the tunnel up toward the entrance, he realized Tyler was right: *no rope!* He traced the path of the yellow rope in the light of his headlamp down into the pit below. *It's all down there on the floor but it's not next to Jamie. That's not possible . . . unless . . .* A sudden and familiar reaction welled up in his chest, that same sensation he'd felt so many times in Afghanistan: *slight fear mixed with powerful anger.* It was a hard emotional mixture to manage but he knew from experience it was more important to focus on what needed to get done—Jamie needed help *and now!*

"Yeah, Tyler, something's not right, but we've got to focus on Jamie." Suddenly the cause of Jamie's fall was obvious: *someone knows we're in here and set this up.*

Tyler was coming to the same conclusion but didn't want to betray his fear to Eric. "I'll handle your safety rope . . . you better get down there." He pulled the first aid kit from the equipment bag. "You're gonna need this." Eric clipped the kit to his belt and Tyler stepped back as far as he could, ready to handle the belay for Eric's descent.

"Now!" Eric said firmly then leaned back over the edge and quickly disappeared as Tyler played out his rope. When it stopped, Eric yelled, "I'm in!" and Tyler tied off the safety line the way Eric had taught him. When it was secure he knelt at the edge of the shaft and trained his light on the floor below where Eric was bent over Jamie.

"How is she, Eric?"

"She's alive. Pretty badly hurt though. She's passed out . . .

and I think her arm and maybe her leg are broken."

The sound of Ryan's footsteps preceded him as he now returned. He stuck his head into the doorway and asked how Jamie was. After a quick update he leaned over to see for himself. "There oughta be some smelling salts in the first aid kit."

"I need you down here, Ryan. She's pretty banged up. Can you climb down the rope without a harness? Just don't you get hurt too, okay?"

"Right! I'm on my way." Ryan put on his gloves, grabbed ahold of the rope, and carefully inched his way down, using a hand-under-hand descent. It reminded him of the tough rope-climbing tests in junior high gym class. At least today he had on leather gloves.

Tyler watched as Eric and Ryan carefully untangled Jamie from the broken boards under her and stretched out her "good" leg before dealing with the one lying at a painfully wrong angle. Eric held smelling salts under her nose and suddenly she shook her head ferociously and screamed. For an instant she paused with fearful eyes but once she recognized who was with her, she began to cry uncontrollably.

"Tyler, go find Mac and see if she's up to coming back, okay?" Eric asked. "We're going to need you and her both!"

"Sure." He stood and headed up the long tunnel toward the entrance and returned with her about ten minutes later.

"How's Jamie?" Mac's voice was composed now and the shock of her own near-fall had subsided. Cautiously she inched to the edge and became upset once again to see Jamie so hurt. Then she remembered something important. "You need to wrap her in that foil micro blanket in the first aid kit. In Girl Scouts they warned us about shock and needing to keep your patient warm." She wiped the corners of her eyes and took a deep breath.

Ryan and Eric had been so busy trying to get Jamie comfortable, they'd forgotten first aid rule number one: prevent shock. "On it!" Ryan called up and began unpacking a silver blanket that looked like flimsy foil, but was capable of retaining a serious amount of body heat. A few minutes passed as they continued to do what they could for Jamie. Finally, Eric stood to estimate the distance up to the top of the pit and assess just how they were going to get Jamie up—and *out* of the mine.

"Mac, we're in quite a jam," Eric finally said, looking up. "What we really need is that winch on the Cruiser. I don't see any other safe way of getting her up. Do you remember how to drive the FJ40 in low four-wheel gear like I taught you over spring break?"

"Yeah . . ." Mac replied tentatively, and suddenly guessed what her uncle wanted.

"Take a quad and find a cell signal and call for help. Then if you think you can make it, I need you to drive the FJ40 up here."

Mac thought of that draw that even Jamie hadn't attempted. "Do you really think I can do it?" She wished she could see Eric's or her dad's eyes. She needed their confidence to try to do what seemed to be an impossible task.

Her dad answered. "It's not going to be easy, Mac. But yes, you can do it. Jamie's counting on you. We've got to get her out of here."

"Do you want me to go with her?" Tyler asked.

"No, we need you down here to help us splint Jamie's leg and arm," answered Eric. "Mac, tell the sheriff that we're up in the north end of Rooster Canyon, just below the microwave tower. Give them the GPS coordinates and tell them we need help with a serious climbing accident, possibly a compound leg and arm fracture. The call's more important than getting back here with the Toyota. But it'll take time for them to get here so if you *can* drive the Cruiser up, it'll help big time, okay?"

"Yes, sir," she said, trying to sound more confident than she really was.

"How about you handle a safety rope for me before you go?" Tyler gave her a wink in the dim light. "And by the way, you know you've got this, Mac. Right? Don't sweat it—just do it. Okay?" He wanted to sound encouraging but he remembered going up that draw earlier today on a four-wheeler. *He was glad they weren't depending on him to bring the Cruiser's winch back up here!*

She smiled back and watched Tyler tie the second rope around his waist and thread it through the carabiner tied to the rail. Holding the main rope he carefully slid over the edge. *Boy, was he glad he'd learned how to climb a rope in gym class!*

When he reached the bottom, Mac tied off the rope and exited the mine as quickly as her headlamp allowed. Within ten minutes she was on the four-wheel ATV making her way back up to the trail. She was nervous but confident that they could depend on her to get help and to get back with the Cruiser. And soon!

31

THE PROFESSOR MAKES HIS MOVE

The professor had waited quietly ever since he'd heard the roar of the scaffolding's collapse rumble deep into the mine. He watched from the darkness as they sent first one, then two of the men down into the pit to check on whoever had fallen through the floor. Now he knew it was that Jamie-person.

It really hadn't been his intent that anyone would follow the yellow rope out far enough out onto the scaffolding to be in danger. He'd only wanted to confuse and delay them. *Scare them off!* But now their Jamie had fallen, and it sounded like she was badly hurt. And he couldn't help but notice that in all the hubbub and confusion, the men had dropped the two boxes and everyone was down in the pit. Except the girl. And she was gone!

He moved silently closer to the first box, which was faintly illuminated by the glow of light coming up from the pit. As he reached out and touched it, he listened as they spoke to Jamie—trying to comfort her and promising her that they would get her out. Something about Mac going to get the Land Cruiser and it would be okay.

He tried to lift the box and realized how heavy it was. It would be easier to drag it, but that would make a lot of noise. He didn't know what was in them, but he suspected it must be something special for them to weigh so much. But how had these people known to look for boxes? And how had they known *where* to look?

"But does that matter now? This is your chance!" his voice whispered to him in the dark. "The girl is gone, but she'll be back. The rest are all in the hole. What are you going to do?"

He looked into the opening and traced the ropes in the pit back to where they were tied on to the rail track. If they heard him, someone would come scrambling up those ropes. He looked again at the two boxes and quickly made up his mind. It was a mean thing to do, but the girl would be back and they'd eventually find their way out. His waiting here wasn't going to help Jamie. "But whatever is in these boxes just might help you!"

Yes, you're right—this just might fix everything, he told himself proudly.

And so, without delay or even a second thought about the havoc and pain he'd already caused, he inched forward on his knees and unclipped the carabiner and head loop from the old iron rail. All the ropes they needed to get out of the pit were attached to this yoke, so unhooking it meant they couldn't come after him. When they pulled on the line, it would come tumbling down around them. He set the loop carefully to the side, almost in the doorway of the side room. Then he stood, took hold of the handle of the box closest to the entry, and began the slow process of dragging it up to the mine's opening.

"Who's up there?" he heard one of them shout. "What's going on up there?" another called. "Hey! who are you and what are you doing?" the boy yelled out. The professor ignored them all. They couldn't see him, only hear him. Why answer? It was pointless. All he planned to do was take *his* boxes from them.

"I'll go up!" one of them hollered. And almost immediately he heard the carabiner scrape along the scaffolding before reaching the end and falling free. There was *lots* more shouting then. But he ignored it all and continued to drag the box closer to the entry, moving faster now as his feet got into a rhythm on the mine's rocky floor.

Out in the light, he quickly looked around. No sign of the girl. Spotting one of the two remaining ATVs, he managed to pull the box over to it and finally, after a few choice words and a smashed finger, was able to heave it up and onto the quad runner's cargo rack. He quickly went back in, now using his flashlight, which made the return trip much easier. As he pulled the second box onto a rail, the noise alerted the trapped group to his return. "What are you doing up there?" one of the voices demanded. "We need your help! Our friend's badly hurt! Are you leaving us down here?"

The question bothered him. It wasn't right to leave them trapped. The right thing would be to help them, but doing the right thing wasn't on his to-do list just now and getting this second box out and onto the ATV was. *Why?* Because whatever was in these boxes was going to make everything okay.

The box shrieked as he began to drag it along the rail. His thoughts turned to his escape. He'd leave El Paso. He'd get away from Tony the Fish. And he'd never, ever have to teach clueless freshman college students ever again! *These boxes had to be full of treasure, right?*

"Our friend is hurt!" the voice shouted again. "You could help us! Why are you leaving us stranded?" And now a second voice: "You've sabotaged our ropes and trapped us down here! Who are you? Why did you want to kill Jamie?"

"I didn't intend to hurt her," the professor replied impulsively before he could stop himself. "She's not dead, is she?" he asked in a sudden panic.

Oops. Not what he'd intended to say! He knew she wasn't dead. They were still talking to her, reassuring her. *It was a trick! Well, it doesn't matter 'cause I'm leavin the mine and then leavin' town, and these boxes are my ticket out!* He resumed dragging the box along the rail. The noise was awful but it moved so much more quickly.

"Who are you? Come back! Help us!" The voices, muted now, echoed eerily from the shaft behind him. But he was already well on his way to the entrance of the mine. He wasn't going to be tricked into talking with them anymore.

He paused to catch his breath once he was back in the sunlight. Dragging these two boxes had left him exhausted. As he struggled to get the second box to the ATV, he considered leaving it and settling for just one . . . until *No, it's going with me!* He groaned and tugged and finally got it on the rack beside the first. He paused long enough to wipe the sweat out of his eyes with his shirtsleeve and cinched the cargo straps. Now to get to his car hidden on the South Trail before the girl got back.

The professor swung his leg across the seat of the ATV and started it up, revving the engine loudly several times. Convinced everything would be better now, he accelerated up the steep trail, the spinning tires tossing gravel as he made his way with his heavy load.

32

TIME TO MOVE OUT

S ometimes things in the surveillance business go crazy all
at once. That was exactly what was about to unfold. "Agent
Ramirez!" Hassan called out. "Quick, have a look at this!"

The two of them watched the video feed from the drone as an
ATV came into view from a sidetrack they'd not noticed before.
It was moving erratically like the cargo rack was overloaded, or
the driver didn't know what he was doing. *Or maybe both.* They
also saw that Gatto and his cowboys had just turned onto this
branch of the trail instead of going straight up the mountain to
the microwave tower. Just then the ATV came around a curve
and almost ran into them. They could hear Gatto yell something
to his cowboys, but it was unintelligible with the wind and the
altitude of the drone. His intent was soon clear enough anyway:
the ATV was blocked. The rider turned off the engine and

stepped off with his hands in the air.

"Let's roll." Harper clapped his hand on Ramirez's shoulder.

David and Matt passed the reins of the extra horses to the two agents and mounted their own. After quick instructions to Hassan, they left their command point and headed up the trail toward the far rim of Rooster Canyon. David took the lead and Matt the rear, as all four set out at a fast but safe pace for themselves and the horses. As they rode, Ramirez continued to glance at the video feed on his phone. He could see that one of the cowboys had now swapped his horse for the ATV and was driving it back down the side trail to wherever it had just come up from. The other cowboy had dismounted and was leading the two horses down the trail behind the skinny man who'd been riding the ATV earlier. Gatto was in the saddle of his horse bringing up the rear.

"Skypants, this is 37," Ramirez said into his walkie-talkie.

"Copy you, 37," Hassan answered. "What's up?"

"Skypants, need a zoom-out on the current ten-twenty."

"10-4, stand by."

As he watched the screen, the image shifted and he could see that Gatto and cowboys were heading into a clearing at the bottom of the hill below them. Suddenly it was obvious where they were all going—an abandoned mine! This was starting to make some sense. Ramirez gave Harper and David an update.

"We can push our way up the trail," David responded. "But at best we're probably twenty-five to thirty minutes out from there."

"Understand." Ramirez got back on the radio. "Skypants, looks like we've got a situation. You're going to have to do a double-trade on that route so we don't lose eyeballs up there. You copy?"

"Copy that, 37. We'll keep a hot-swap at all times till you let us know otherwise," Hassan replied.

This meant there would be a drone on-station at all times, even though it would require more round-trip flights to make that happen. Hurry up and wait had suddenly turned into simply *hurry up!*

33

PLANNING FOR
THE IMPOSSIBLE

By the time she'd driven about a mile along the canyon ledge, Mackenzie finally had a cell signal. She stopped and called the sheriff's department and briefly explained what had happened and gave them the coordinates for the mine. The friendly dispatcher knew exactly where she was talking about. She assured Mac that they'd get medical help up to them as quickly as possible, but it could take possibly as long as two hours, given the remote location and the need for a helicopter.

Mackenzie continued along the ridge until she finally came to the top of the draw. From where she stood, she could see where Jamie had parked the Cruiser at the bottom. She could also make out a few scattered elements of the original trail and its switchbacks, but rainstorms, rockslides, boulder debris and washouts had ruined this portion long ago. She figured she'd better plan how to attack it now—especially from such a great vantage point.

If she started at the bottom by following the original lay of the trail across the face of the draw, she could see where she'd be risking some sideways slide about midways across. But if she could be gutsy and accelerate and shoot past that gap, the left edge would be a safe enough place to pause . . . So that would be her first objective—her first "gate." And that would line her up for the next challenge: the biggest washout of the hill. She decided she'd just have to take that one head on and hope she didn't stall. If she could make it up and out of that washout near its top, that would be her second gate. It was the riskiest place for a stall but it was also what the slow, tractor-like, four-wheel low gear was best at.

Next another turn, and then she'd have to scale two boulders in order to cross the face. They blocked what would otherwise be a straight shot across to a ledge from the original trail. There was a gnarly tree on the far side if she made it. She decided the boulders were gate three.

The next washout, which was over halfway up the draw, wasn't as bad as the first one, so that would be her fourth gate. But now it got tricky. From there a quad could do a quick scramble up the last part and be done, but the angle of attack for the Cruiser was too steep. That meant having to cross the draw once more and the only path possible would take the driver's side tires over the largest boulder on the face of the hillside. Get the line wrong and the Cruiser could tip and roll over onto the passenger side and she'd be stuck. Worse, take the boulder wrong the other way and she'd be high-centered and marooned on top of it.

Either mistake would mean a failure to get the winch back to the mine. She remembered the old *Apollo 13* movie with Tom Hanks, then told herself out loud, "Failure is not an option, gentlemen!" It made her laugh at the thought of mission control running this rescue from Houston. *But this is all on me.* She was beginning to appreciate why Jamie parked the Cruiser and hitched a ride on the quad. *What have I gotten myself into?*

She surveyed the climb one last time before carefully easing the ATV into a cautious, downhill descent. When she reached the bottom she looked back up. This was going to be nearly impossible. Throttling the quad she drove to a large boulder between her and the Cruiser, shut it down, and stepped off. Her whole body was tense from the descent and nervousness about what she had to do. *First things first!* She lifted the seat and hid the key where Eric always kept his spare.

Time to rescue Jamie! She took two steps toward the Cruiser, glanced down, and froze. Near a clump of tall grasses alongside a large boulder, a large rattlesnake lay coiled between her and the truck. She heard its frighteningly soft rattle as it eyed her, ready to strike. Two more steps and it surely would have sunk its fangs into her leg. Mac caught her breath as she stared back at the snake for a moment that seemed to last forever. *Quick! What to do?*

Back up—slowly . . . she began to step backwards in slow motion . . . inching her way to the ATV. Then the snake suddenly uncoiled and slithered away. She was relieved—but only for only a moment—it had slithered its way under the Cruiser!

Mac had seen only one other rattler and that was at the ranch. She'd been with Eric and Jamie, and Jamie'd almost stepped in front of one. It too had been coiled, and Eric told them to quickly back up and give the snake plenty of room to make its getaway. That's when he told her that snakes don't like noise. *Noise!* She reached over to the handlebar of the ATV and pushed the horn button as long and frequently as she could. When she calmed down she stopped and took a deep breath. *Surely it's not under the truck anymore . . . right?* Why would it stick around with such a racket? She stood up and began to boldly walk toward the Cruiser. *No snake in sight so far.*

About seven or eight feet away, she cautiously squatted down to get a look underneath. It was pretty dark, but nothing moved or looked like a stick or a snake. Convincing herself once more that the rattler had kept on going, she decided to make a quick dash and leap up on the step rail.

Fixing her eyes on the door, she took four long steps; and grabbing the handle as she jumped, she opened the door, slid into the seat, and slammed the door shut . . . all with no snake! Still, she was shaking as she squeezed the steering wheel with both hands and took deep breaths to calm herself. *It's going to be okay. That snake was out there but she was safe in here.*

34

TRAPPED

C hris-the-Cat watched the professor walking ahead of the group as they headed to the mine and realized he was in a jam. He was good at anticipating challenges and having a contingency planned for most any scenario, but he was suddenly unsure of what to do next. He'd anticipated the possibility of finding the professor up here but not interrupting his escape on a four-wheeler with two Old West strong boxes in tow.

On the other hand, he *had* anticipated having to do something drastic—something unfriendly, like dumping the helpful cowboy guides. That was why he'd quietly activated a map tracker app on his cell phone when they started out earlier and why he'd made careful note of how they'd gotten here. There had always been the possibility that he'd have to leave the cowboys behind when he got here.

As they reached the clearing and could see the mine, he decided to play things cordial for now. "That's fine, Eddie. You can just park the ATV right there. This here is a former business associate of mine . . . we just need to have a brief chat." He turned to face the professor from his seat high up in the saddle and grinned at the frightened man below. "So good to see you again, Professor," he said politely, as if they were a couple of old colleagues running into each other at Starbucks.

The professor wasn't so sure they were friends. "Uhh, hi there, Mister Chris. Uhh, kinda funny running into you up here," he mumbled. He looked back and forth between Gatto on the horse and the two cowboys off to the side, holding the reins of their horses, waiting to see exactly what was going on.

But Gatto could sense the professor's concern about talking in front of strangers and quickly decided to leave Eddie and his friend out of this. "Boys, I wonder if you could give the professor and me some space for a private conversation. You okay with that?" He spoke with the silky sincerity of a great white shark dressed in a tuxedo.

"Sure, man." Eddie put his Stetson back on and turned to his friend. "Whatcha say, Roland? How 'bout we walk the horses up here a spell." He gave a light tug on the reins and the two men sauntered to the far side of the clearing to where the trail led up the hill.

Gatto watched them before turning back to the professor. "So, Professor, looks like you've had a very successful adventure up here in these mountains." He took off his hat and wiped the sweat from his forehead. "How 'bout you tell me about these two handsome boxes you've got there."

"I, uhh, well . . . I kinda found them down there in the mine," he stammered. It was a challenge to look up at Gatto with the sun coming over his shoulder. He looked toward the boxes instead. "It's not the ore I thought I'd find, but these boxes sure looked sharp. Thought they'd make a nice souvenir of the expedition." He was trying to make up anything that might prevent having to open them.

"I'd love to believe you, Professor. Really would." Gatto's smile never changed. "But the problem is that you're about a week late on your loan." He paused. "I'm pretty sure that you don't have several hundred thousand dollars' worth of high grade silver ore in those two boxes there—am I right?" Gatto leaned forward menacingly in his saddle.

His smile instantly disappeared and he growled in a menacing voice: "A little birdie tells me you ain't found nothin' in the way of silver ore." He waited to let the professor squirm some more. "And that's kind of a problem for our business deal, Professor, don't you think?" He sat back up in the saddle and looked at the hot sky. "So, Professor," he finally said after an uncomfortably long pause, "how 'bout you showing me what's in those boxes? Who knows—maybe we'll find something that will settle you up with Tony."

"Well, uhh . . . I honestly don't know what's in them, Mr. Chris," he half-mumbled, struggling to come up with a believable story. "You see, they're locked and all, so I was going to take them to the university and have them looked over by one of my archeologist friends." He tried to make a convincing smile but it looked pathetic, more like utter panic.

Gatto climbed off his horse and walked over to the boxes and the professor backed up to give him plenty of room. Circling them slowly, he said, "I think you're lying to me, Professor. I'm not a very patient person when someone lies to me."

"Honest, Mr. Chris," he stammered quickly now, growing more fearful. "I've got no idea what's in 'em. I'd be happy to split whatever's there with you and Mr. Tony if you let me take them back to the university." He looked at the boxes and then back to Gatto.

Gatto put his smile back on and turned to call out to the cowboys. "Hey guys!" Eddie and Roland, who were trying to ignore the conversation across the clearing from them, saw Gatto motion them to come back. "I assume both of you carry a firearm, right?" He knew no self-respecting Texas rancher or cowboy would not have their concealed carry license for a pistol of some sort.

"Sure." They looked at each other and back at Gatto. "Why?" Eddie asked.

"Well, you know how in the movies the hero uses his gun to shoot the lock off of a box? Can you help us get these boxes open?"

Eddie shook his head. "That's cowboy movie mythology, man!" he grinned. "You go shooting a 9mm slug at a piece of heavy steel like that lock and you're pretty likely to get hit by a ricocheting bullet."

"I knew a kid back in high school who actually tried it and lost his foot," Roland chimed in.

"Shame." Gatto looked around the clearing and happened to spot the crowbar that Eric and Ryan had left behind after they'd pried the boards off the front of the mine, and then noticed the boards themselves. Suddenly a better solution to his dilemma came to mind. "Well, dang," he said with mock frustration. "Guess we'll have to use a crowbar." Looking very appreciative and sincere he added, "I'm sure glad I wasn't carrying today—I'd have gone off and done something stupid and probably blown my toes off!" He laughed at himself and playfully punched Roland on the shoulder, and the cowboys quickly joined in, breaking the tension.

City slickers just don't know the things a man oughta know! Roland thought as he watched Gatto.

Gatto suggested to the professor that he look around to see if he could find a crowbar then turned again to cowboys. "Roland," he began, pretending to be naïve, "you obviously know more than I do about firearms, so maybe you can give me some advice while we're waiting."

"Sure. What's up?"

"Well, a friend was telling me about a pistol called a SNUG, or something like that. He and I, well, we're getting ready to take our concealed carry course and he says that's the weapon we should buy to qualify with. What do you think? Is that what you carry?"

Predictably, Roland reached behind him and drew his pistol from his back belt holster, proud to show it to Gatto. "Naw, I know it's old fashioned, but personally, I prefer a Smith & Wesson .38. Closest thing to an old Colt Six-Shooter—like real cowboys used to carry."

Gatto held out his hand. "Mind if I have a look? My best friend had almost convinced me, but maybe I should consider a .38 for our CCL course instead. I guess an old police revolver never occurred to me . . . Are those real pearl handles?"

Convinced this was a casual conversation between men who appreciated a fine firearm, Roland was excited to tell Gatto about his .38. "You bet—they're mother of pearl! It's an authentic police issue my grandfather used to carry. He was a detective in El Paso in the 50s." He opened the revolver and emptied the rounds into the palm of his hand, then passed it to Gatto so he could have a closer look.

Immediately Gatto casually leaned over, and before anyone recognized what was happening, he was holding a high-power automatic pistol he'd just pulled from his boot. "Let's have it,

181

Eddie—would love to see yours as well. Simple request, Eddie. Nothing funny and no one gets hurt." The threat in his voice and demeanor left nothing to the imagination. "Try to be a hero and you're dead. Okay?"

Eddie was furious but had no choice but to give his pistol to the city boy from El Paso.

"Thanks." Gatto tucked Eddie's gun away. "So, friends, this here is the professor." Gatto gestured with the tip of his pistol to the professor, who was standing off to the side, waiting to be summoned. "And . . . well . . . the whole reason we're out here today is because he's come up a bit short on a payment to a friend of mine. We thought he might be hiding out up here in the mountains." He glanced over to the ATV and the sinister smile returned to his face. "But the professor here, he's agreed to trade me these two boxes as a down payment on his tab."

He paused and again pointed to him with his weapon. "Only problem, you see, is I don't trust that he won't change his mind on our way back to El Paso so I'm going to ask him to wait here at the mine while I head home. It might be a bit of a long wait, I know, but I've promised him I'll call the authorities when I get back and provide an anonymous tip that our friend here has gotten himself lost up in the mountains."

Gatto glanced over to the cowboys. "A reasonable idea . . . don't you think?" Without waiting for an answer to a question that really wasn't a question, he continued. "And if you don't mind—and I'm certain you won't—I need to ask for your help boarding up that entry over there, with the professor on the other side, of course."

With the pistol in Gatto's hand, Eddie and Roland realized they had no choice.

"Yeah, right," Eddie mumbled with a sneer.

After all but the top two boards had been nailed on, Gatto

instructed the professor to climb over and into the mine. Next Gatto turned to the cowboys. "You guys too," he ordered, again motioning with the pistol for emphasis. "You boys can keep him company this afternoon." Reluctantly, they did as they were told.

When all three men were inside and had stepped back as instructed, Gatto finished nailing the final two boards in place and tossed the hammer to the side of the entrance. Then he heard Eddie speaking in a soft but bold tone: "Best you not harm those horses, Mr. Gatto. If I get out of here and find you've hurt them, I swear I will hunt you down if it's the last thing I do."

Gatto wasn't used to threats coming from someone who held no cards. All the same, he was impressed by Eddie's courage. "I do respect and admire a man who knows his horses," Gatto responded, with true sincerity this time. "I can tie them to the boards here if you like or I can tie their reins to their saddles and let them go free. What's your preference?"

Set them free was the reply. Gatto agreed and returned his pistol to his concealed holster and started to the professor's ATV. Halfway there he stopped, turned, and strode back to the mine. "Eddie, it's been a pleasure working with you and Roland," he said with a mix of sincerity and firmness. "And I'm so very sorry about having to inconvenience you and Roland this afternoon. But all the same, if you ever do come looking for me . . ." and now his smile disappeared as he finished in a steely voice, "well, rest assured, it certainly *will* be the last thing you do. Got that?"

Grinning smugly, Gatto climbed on the quad runner and revved up the engine. Spinning a terrible cloud of gravel and dust, he headed up the steep trail to return the way they had come.

35

A CLUTCH, A 5-SPEED, AND 4WD-LOW

E ventually, after five or ten minutes, Mac stopped thinking about the snake and remembered the reason she'd come back for the Cruiser: *Time to rescue Jamie!* She retrieved the keys from under the sun visor, depressed the clutch, put the gear shift into neutral, and started the motor to let it warm up. As she watched the tachometer on the dash showing the engine RPMs, she tried to remember all the things Eric had taught her that spring about rock climbing in a 4WD.

"You don't want the motor to stall—so let it idle and get fully warmed up since it's going to be working hard in low gear." She remembered the odd sensation of them crawling along so very slowly but not killing the motor. "Give it enough gas to keep it moving," he'd said. *"Keep It Moving! K—I—M . . . remember KIM!"*

"Remember KIM!" she said loudly, "Keep It Moving!" Between most of the gates, she'd want to keep the Cruiser moving. She looked up the draw and rehearsed her plan once more—gate by gate. "Now or never!" she announced and stepped on the clutch pedal, shifted into first gear, and gave it some gas. But the Cruiser simply lurched and died—she'd let the clutch out too fast and stalled the motor.

"Not a great start, Mac!" she scolded. "Jamie's depending on you, so get yourself together and get it done!"

She restarted the motor and tried again, but once more it stalled. She started to tear up and suddenly collapsed, "I can't even get started . . . how am I going to get up that hill?" she screamed to the rocks. Somehow in her frustration, she remembered the transfer case and could hear Eric as if he were here: "If you're going to tackle a true rock climb, you'll use four-low, not four-high. So if the hubs are already locked, move the transfer lever from four-high to four-low." She looked at the lever . . . sure enough, it was still in four-high!

"Duh!" Mac shook her head, reached down, and moved it into low. She rehearsed the clutch and gas thing one more time. *The clutch and gas pedal work together. The gas revs up as the clutch eases in. The clutch connects the motor to the gearbox and the gears drive the wheels. Gas pedal down, clutch pedal up . . . just like a seesaw.*

"I've got this!" She concentrated on listening for the right tone of the motor and feeling the right resistance of the clutch against her foot, and this time the Cruiser lurched briefly but kept rolling. *Finally! This is really happening!* She glanced at the hill to spot her first gate and steered to where she intended to line up to start the climb.

"Just go from gate-to-gate," she told herself and scanned the ground in front of her. "The *climb* may look impossible, but none of the individual pieces are impossible. Complete all five gates and you'll be up on the ridge!" She took a deep breath, gave the Cruiser some gas and pointed it up and across the hill. As the front and back tires took turns going up then back down several big rocks, lifting and lowering the Cruiser, it reminded her of a carnival ride at the state fair. She felt the tires pull at the wheel as it clambered along, but she hung on tight, determined to stay in control. *I'm the captain of this four-wheel ride!*

As the back tire rolled off yet another small boulder, Mac steered hard to the right. Time to line up for the race up and across the face. A wide patch of loose gravel and debris littered this part, just as it started to get steeper. But Mac's plan was good and the Cruiser was making progress—slow but deliberate, and she hadn't lost traction yet. Then halfway across, the cruiser began to slip sideways. The tires didn't spin . . . but the sensation of sliding sideways startled her.

Time to make her move. She could hear Eric once more: "Sometimes speed and risk can pay off in loose rocks. Speed sounds counterintuitive, but a sprint across a loose surface can beat the slide of gravity . . ." She tried to ignore the rest of the sentence: ". . . not always, but if you do it just right, that move may surprise you." Mac slowly accelerated. There was a moment when one of the front tires lost traction, but the other three held, and she could sense that the speed was allowing her to cover more ground even though the Cruiser continued to slip and grab. She'd almost made it to her first gate, when the angle of the slope became too great and gravel began spinning from under the left rear tire. Instinctively she jerked the wheel to the left to turn into the slide and then accelerated. She was surprised and relieved as all four tires caught and the Cruiser

187

cleared the last of the debris field. She paused at the edge of the draw to look back at what she'd accomplished and nodded with approval. *Good job! Gate one complete.*

The long washout she'd surveyed from above led to gate two. This was going to be just like the bottom of the draw— bumping up and over lots of rocks, but this time all uphill. At least these weren't loose. They'd been exposed as rains washed away the ground cover, but most were still firmly embedded in the hillside. She plotted her path. There were a couple of big rocks to avoid and a few places where she could accelerate and gain some momentum. Convinced she was ready, Mac shoved the tall shift lever into gear and pressed the gas pedal lightly as she let out the clutch. The Cruiser surged forward up the draw. *Keep It Moving!*

This part was going to be straight uphill. *Can the Cruiser really do this?* She gripped the steering wheel, fighting each rock that tried to take control. She'd made it over halfway up the washout when suddenly, just as she rolled off a big rock and tried to accelerate, the motor stalled and quit and the Cruiser began to roll backward. She slammed her foot onto the brake pedal, and the truck held.

The sudden change of momentum and silence frightened her. Looking over her shoulder, she saw how far up the draw she'd come. But looking back was a mistake because it made her only more aware of her precarious situation. The tears she'd fought back earlier now flooded out and she sobbed for a minute or more, totally unnerved by what had just happened.

"I can't do this!" She yelled out the window, tears stinging her cheeks. "I can't get this done. I'm stuck. I never should've tried this!" The shrill blare of a horn startled her as she collapsed onto the steering wheel crying and her forehead bumped the button in the center. She jumped and instantly regained her focus. After blinking away tears and wiping her eyes on the sleeves of her tee shirt, she sniffed and peered ahead through the windshield.

What would Eric do? She set the gear in reverse, pulled on the brake, and climbed out. She needed to see the situation from the ground and was surprised to find that just ahead, it was almost flat for about the length of the Cruiser. "All I need right here, right now, is just two feet forward!"

When she looked behind her, she realized that backing down and starting over was not an option. Then she noticed some rocks that were big, but not too big for her to move. An idea clicked, and ten minutes later she'd managed to roll, lift, and drag enough of them to firmly block the back tires so she couldn't roll backwards. Surely now the Cruiser could make it two feet.

She climbed in and found herself saying a short prayer her mom had taught her when she was little. Then she pushed in the clutch, started the engine, and announced to the mirror, "Show time! . . . First gear, gas, and slowly let out the clutch." The back tires started to spin but then grabbed the rocks and held long enough for all four wheels to move forward. *Crisis conquered!* She blinked and took a deep breath. Onward to the goal: the top of the washout.

With gate two complete, Mac was able to navigate the easiest crossing of the draw, which got her to gate three and the gnarly old tree. Pleased with her progress, she headed up the next washout, which wasn't as long or as steep as the first. When she made it to gate four, she was starting to feel more confident, so she stopped, shifted into neutral, pulled on the handbrake, and stepped out to assess what she'd accomplished so far. As she looked down the hill she felt a rush of self-pride and excitement—and disbelief at how steep that climb had been. *And now I'm almost to the top!*

Gate five, her final challenge, lay before her. Much of the original track up here was still useful, but there was a serious washout to deal with and a giant boulder about the size her tires. She couldn't go around it—the slope was too steep above and below. She could see that her original plan was still the right way to handle this last twenty yards. Aim the driver's side tires up and over the boulder just right and straddle both it and the hillside at the same time. It had to be a perfect line! If the Cruiser didn't climb the rock just right, it would tip and roll onto the passenger side, and she'd be marooned.

She climbed back in and got ready. When she glanced to her left and realized how far it was to the bottom, she almost lost her nerve, but suddenly she remembered something her dad had told her when she was four and learning to ride a bike. "Look straight ahead, Mac. Don't look to the left or right, you might crash . . . just keep looking ahead at where you want to go." It was good advice she needed right now. She fixed her eyes on the exact balance point on the boulder and started to inch forward. "Here we go!" she said softly.

The first ten yards were easier than she'd imagined, but getting the Cruiser up and onto the boulder was tricky. The hillside wanted to pull one way and the tire had its own ideas. *Hands tight. Don't lose your grip. Just let the Cruiser pull itself over the rock.* She continued fighting to control the steering wheel while inching forward . . . and the next thing she knew, the tire was rolling down the far side of the rock. *Now for the back.* She adjusted the wheel slightly to make sure the Cruiser didn't miss its line, and moments later the back tire also rolled off. *Success!*

"Mackenzie Foster—five, boulders—zero! Try and beat that!" She raised a fist of triumph in the air but realized she couldn't stop and celebrate just yet. She aimed more to the right and up the face to finish the sprint to the other side of the washout. *A little more gas.* One tire briefly lost traction and spun gravel, but she focused on steering hard right. Then, leaving gate five behind and reaching the top rim of the draw she gave the gas pedal a slight tap and felt the front end lift into the air for a moment, then settle onto its two front tires. The back tires followed and the Cruiser was suddenly horizontal once more – a strange sensation after riding at such odd angles all the way up. When she'd rolled another fifteen feet forward she stopped, exhausted but thrilled.

"I did it! I did it! I won!" Mac grinned triumphantly, as she pounded the steering wheel and honked the horn. Then her flushed cheeks begin to tingle and she realized she was crying again. This time, however, they weren't tears of frustration, these were from satisfaction and amazement. She'd done the impossible! She pulled on the brake and let the Cruiser idle as she got out to stretch her legs and relax her quivering arms. Her hands and fingers ached from gripping the steering wheel so tightly. Shaking them vigorously, she walked over to look down the draw—and she couldn't believe what she'd just done. The slope was so incredibly steep!

It struck her that so many things could have gone wrong —*disastrously wrong!* It was a sudden, humbling thought that reminded her there was so much more than just her own little ability that enabled her to made it to the top. Mac closed her eyes for a moment and whispered a prayer of thanksgiving, then turned and took in the amazing view out across the canyon. For a moment she felt like she was in a movie with grand, heroic music in the background. What would her dad think? Her mom and Eric? She grinned as she tried to imagine Tyler's reaction if he were here. And at that moment, in spite of the heat, a chill climbed her spine and she rubbed her arms.

Suddenly the image of Jamie lying injured on the floor of the mine shaft invaded her thoughts.

I'm not done yet. I've gotta get going, now. Time to get the Cruiser and the winch up to the mine.

36

GET THE BIRD UP!

Ramirez was furious at what he saw unfolding in the clearing near the mine entry as he watched the remote video feed. He was also second-guessing his own judgment. He never should have allowed such a physical gap between himself and Gatto. Video surveillance like this wasn't the same as being on the other side of a wall or across the street where you could move in fast!

"Our subject's on the move again," he relayed to Harper on the horse in front of him. "He's left the clearing on the ATV they intercepted. I presume he's headed back our way."

"He's a cold one," Harper commented. It hadn't surprised him that Gatto would leave David's son-in-law and the other two men trapped in the mine. *Lucky for them that Chris Gatto had been under FBI surveillance today!*

"Let's call for backup," Ramirez added. "He pulled a gun to force those three into the mine. He's armed and we need to be prepared for a dangerous encounter."

"Agreed." Harper pulled out the high-frequency radio. "Base, this is 37—37 calling Base, over?"

"Go 37."

"Base, we've got a potential shooter under surveillance and headed our way. Suspect in our surveillance warrant and potential shooter are one and the same. Given the remote nature of this location, I'm requesting deployment of the bird we've got on standby. You copy that?"

"Copy, 37. Potential shooter approaching your position and requesting launch of chopper 9-2-9. Confirm. Over."

"Roger, that. Also need an ETA from 9-2-9 once airborne—potential critical timeline. Over."

"10-4, 37. Understand 9-2-9 is to contact you on this frequency when airborne with ETA. Base out."

Ramirez looked at his watch. "This was an assigned backup, so the bird's been on standby. You think eighteen minutes or so to get here?"

"I'd be surprised if it took them more than twelve."

"Even better. Ask David to pull up and let's have a brief talk." Harper glanced at the monitor. "We need a plan that works for this trail. We may not have twelve minutes before Gatto gets down here now that he's got a quad runner!"

Ramirez brought David and Matt up to speed on what had happened to Roland and Eddie but emphasized that they appeared to be unharmed. Their suspect was headed back down the trail on an ATV, armed and potentially dangerous. If the chopper didn't show up in time, their rules of engagement presumed they would do what they could to avoid a shoot-out but things could escalate in a hurry.

It was Matt who suggested an ambush at a place they'd passed about a quarter of a mile back. The trail at that point made a sharp bend as it dropped down from the ridge. Since a rider's line of sight would be pretty restricted coming down the mountain, they could create a debris field that he wouldn't see until he'd negotiated the turn—and by then it would be too late to avoid it.

"You sound experienced in this kind of action," Harper observed, approving of the plan.

"You learn a lot in the mountains of Afghanistan as an Army Ranger," he replied with a confident and knowing grin.

Harper simply smiled and nodded his head. "Okay, then, let's get back down there. We've got a trap to set!

37

MAC TO THE RESCUE

The flat trail along the side of the mountain should have been the easiest part of Mac's job to get the Cruiser and its winch to the mine. But it wasn't. Although she was safely up on the shelf trail, Mac couldn't draw her eyes away from the edge with its 300-foot drop. And even though she was on the far left and well away from it, she started to panic. *What if I get too close to the edge? What if I lurch to the right and can't control the Cruiser?* Fear seized her. Her heart raced and for a moment she thought she might pass out.

The wind blowing up from the canyon below gusted through the windows of the Cruiser, causing Mac to blink. She shook her head and rubbed her nose to keep from sneezing. *This is silly.* She looked beyond the canyon to the ridgeline in the distance. *Of course I can do this!* She stopped the Cruiser, pulled the gearshift lever back to neutral and carefully let out the clutch, half afraid she'd stall. When nothing bad happened and the motor continued to idle, she set the emergency brake, took her hands off the wheel, and closed her eyes.

She took several deep breaths and suddenly remembered a verse that one of her teachers had taught her years ago when she was in second grade: *Anytime I'm afraid, I will trust in You.* Immediately she sensed a peace and reassurance. *Mackenzie Foster, you just drove a four-wheel-drive Toyota Land Cruiser up an Impossible Crawl all by yourself. You've already done the impossible! Now, Jamie and the others are counting on you. That's what really matters . . . so buck up and finish the job!*

She opened her eyes. The drop-off was still there as well as a terrible sense of what could happen if she got too close, but she also could see that the trail was at least twice as wide as the Toyota—probably even three times as wide for most of the way. She'd drive along the left side, hugging the mountain, and look straight ahead—not down!

I can do this!

Mac nodded as if to confirm to herself that she was ready. She pushed in the clutch, moved the transfer case lever into four-high, and shifted into first gear. As she eased out the clutch, she touched the gas pedal lightly and the Cruiser began rolling forward. When the engine had revved high enough, Mac shifted into second like Eric had taught her. She knew she could easily control her speed if she stayed in second. It wasn't important to go fast—just keep it moving and anticipate the curves!

The shelf trail wasn't more than two or three miles long but it meandered left and right following the contours of the mountain. Sometimes you could see quite a ways ahead, and other times you were in the inside elbow of the mountain terrain. Slowly she made her way, looking to her right only a few times, and each time she did, she became more confident than before. But it was slow going. What seemed like a short distance on the ATV was actually longer than she remembered. Each time she rounded a turn, she thought she must be almost there . . . and then yet another switchback would appear ahead. Finally she spotted a fork up ahead. The left side went up to the microwave tower and the turnoff to the mine while the right one continued twisting in and around the mountain toward the far rim.

Turning left meant another steep, low-gear climb. Once more she engaged the four-low transfer case and then downshifted into first. The truck began another tractor-like crawl as she gave it just enough gas to *Keep It Moving*. Slowly, the Cruiser ascended the steep trail as Mac gripped the steering wheel to guide it over small rocks and washouts. Then just as she turned right to begin the descent to the mine, something caught her eye. It was in the sky, moving—just visible in the corner of the passenger side front windshield. She told herself not to be distracted and keep her focus on the trail, but the object kept drawing her eyes.

Another quick glance and she knew exactly what she was looking at. It was larger than hers, but she knew it was a drone. But what was it doing up here? Suddenly, it blew apart in a cloud of smoke and flying parts and an instant later a gunshot echoed across and along the canyon. She was so startled she almost hit the brakes, but she kept her nerve and watched the last few pieces drift from sky and fall below the trees to the right.

What's a drone doing up here? More importantly . . . what just happened?

38

A VERY LUCKY BREAK

I t was clear to Ramirez that Matt and David knew every yard
and every turn of the Rooster Canyon trail. Once they got
to the blind choke point above the switchback, Ramirez
could see why Matt recommended it as perfect for the ambush.
Certain that Gatto should be reaching the first set of switch
backs beyond the microwave trail, he pulled out his screen
to watch the video feed. But before he could swipe it open, a
gunshot resounded off the walls of the canyon, and when it did
come up, the video feed was solid gray.

"Skypants, 37! What on earth just happened?" shouted
Ramirez into his walkie-talkie as he and Harper dismounted to
scan for the source of the gunshot.

"You missed it?"

"Missed what?"

"Your target spotted our bird! He looked at it, pulled out a pistol and took aim, and next thing the signal went cold. He just shot it out of the air, sir!"

"Not good," Ramirez muttered.

"Active shooter?" Harper continued to scan the walls of the canyon.

"Not at the mine, on the trail. Gatto spotted the bird and took it out in a single shot."

Harper let out a whistle. "Not sure I could do that without a shotgun. Heck-of-a deadeye aim. We better be ready for trouble at the pinch point. He might come up shooting."

"Go ahead on up the ridge and stake out your sight line for the intercept and keep us covered until I've got him tagged." Ramirez looked around for Matt and David. "Have them get those horses somewhere safe and stay out of sight."

"Skypants, you got another bird ready to go?"

"Negative. The dead bird was new on station and the other drone is still returning, and at 20 percent I can't send it back yet. You're going to be running blind, sir," Hassan reported.

"Copy that. But get that bird back up ASAP! I need cover up here as soon as you can. You copy that?"

"Copy. But be advised, ETA is still eight minutes out on Bird 2. Changing batteries and getting it back up to your coordinates isn't going to happen in less than fourteen minutes."

"Roger that," Ramirez replied, concerned that now they really were going into this ambush blind. There was no telling how quickly Gatto would get here, and apart from hearing him coming, they'd have very little time to react. Worse, what if he'd turned around when he saw the drone and was headed back to the mine.

They quickly decided that it was more likely he'd opt for a getaway, so they should go ahead and set up the trap. David and

Matt helped roll several large rocks down the hillside and onto this narrow part of the trail. It didn't take long to have enough debris to make it impossible to continue.

Ramirez found a good position behind rocks about twenty yards directly in front of the ambush field and set up his rifle and scope. His job would be to quickly take out at least one if not both of the front tires of the ATV as soon as it came to a stop. Harper was on the hill directly above and behind the choke point. He made his position behind some boulders to act as backup in case Gatto decided to start shooting. Through his spotting scope he could see Ramirez was in position too.

Just as Ramirez had lined up his scope to his intended target visual, his radio crackled: "The bird just radioed in. They're on a delay/standby," Harper said in his earpiece. "No video stream and active shooter means they're on a brief station-hold confirming new authorizations."

"Copy that," Ramirez replied. "Sounds like it's just us then. You still a go for an intercept here?" He could now hear the whine of the quad runner as it downshifted to slow itself for the upcoming curves.

"He's coming our way," Harper said. "We're a go for closure."

Ramirez turned his attention to the scope on his rifle; he'd have a split-second to nail the inside front tire. The ATV slowed as Gatto rounded the curve and the left front tire was about to enter the crosshairs of his scope when he saw something move on the hill above the trail, up where their guides had taken cover.

Dang! He cursed as he aborted his shot. *Not safe now!* Looking up, he saw David, their trail guide, with the noose of his lasso slowly turning and expanding in the air above him. Then as he extended his arm, the loop floated down and around Gatto's shoulders and arms, and with a simple tug, David hauled

Gatto from the ATV onto the ground.

The unmanned ATV, now without throttle, careened to the left into the wall beside the trail and flipped on its back, leaving the two boxes dangling precariously upside down, held in place only by the cargo strap.

In the same moment, Harper sprang from his position and scrambled down the hillside—half trotting, half sliding—to where Gatto lay squirming on the ground, trying to free himself from the cowboy's rope. While Ramirez hustled over to join his partner, David and Matt worked their way down the hill. Then in a single swift motion, Harper rolled Gatto over and locked handcuffs on his wrists, and with similar speed and precision, frisked him and collected three pistols and a switchblade knife.

David was coiling his rope when Ramirez finally arrived to assist his partner. "Appreciate your help, David, but you could have gotten yourself shot there at that last moment," Ramirez said curtly, as he helped Harper untangle Gatto from the lasso.

"Sorry for the surprise, but it's just the cowboy code." David paused and glared at Gatto. "You don't take what isn't yours and you sure don't mess with another man's family!" He left no doubt that Chris Gatto was lucky to be alive.

Harper got out his radio. "Nine-two-nine, 37. Scene secure, and we need backup," he reported as he surveyed the trail and the overturned ATV.

"Copy that, 37. We've been cleared to the scene after the medivac airspace hold is opened."

"What medivac?"

"An air ambulance out of El Paso has this airspace on hold for approach. We're working to get additional info but until then we're on a static hold twelve minutes out from your coordinates. Copy that?"

"Roger, 9-2-9. Advise when you're released to site. We've got cargo for you and some unfinished business in the upper part of the canyon near an old mine."

"Come again, 37? OP center said something about a mine when they were asking about that medical chopper en route."

Harper got Hassan on the radio so he and the pilot could coordinate the location of the mine. Neither could figure who could have called for a medivac. Meanwhile, Ramirez and the two cowboys managed to roll the ATV back on its tires and tried starting it. Amazingly, it cranked right up. Ramirez was anxious to get to the mine and free David's son-in-law Eddie and his friend Roland. He also wanted to know the identity of the skinny guy also being held in there, the guy Gatto had taken the ATV and the boxes from.

But that would have to wait. With no chopper and a dangerous suspect to secure, rescuing the three was just going to have to wait.

39

A WINCH IS A
WONDERFUL THING

Mackenzie finally turned into the clearing in front of the mine and checked her watch— she'd been gone just a little over an hour but it seemed like half a day. Her arms were sore and tense, plus she was anxious to get out of the Cruiser and be done with the rescue. Of course, she still had to figure out how to get the winch line to Eric and tell everyone about the four-wheel climb up the ravine, and . . . she suddenly stopped thinking of what needed to be done and stared at the mine entrance. Was she imagining things? The entrance was boarded up just like when they'd arrived. She put the transmission in neutral and set the parking brake, but left the motor running as she opened the door and stood on the step rail to size up the situation. Immediately she heard voices she didn't recognize calling out to her.

"Help! Hey, you! Help! You gotta help us get out of here! Help! Please!"

What's going on? Who are these people? Mac was hesitant to move from the safety of the Cruiser but decided to at least drive closer for a better look. Once again, she left the motor running and stood perched on the door frame to see who they were.

"Come on, help us out! Get us out of here!" a man called out desperately. Two or three arms pushed between the boards, waving frantically. Mac scanned the edges of the clearing and the rocks above to see if this was some kind of a trap. *When in doubt, ask a question.* That's what her grandpa had taught her when she was little. *Why not?*

"Who are you and how did you get boarded up in there? And where's my dad and Tyler and Jamie? And Eric!" she added quickly.

"Haven't got a clue who you're talking about, but did you see that guy on the ATV? Did you pass him on the trail?" one man asked. Mac glanced around again and noticed there was only one ATV.

"He just made off with some boxes from this guy who's stuck in here with us," a second voice said. "He forced us in here—his pistol was very persuasive!"

"My family's at the bottom of a mine shaft in there," Mac responded, still unsure whether these were good guys or bad guys.

"I know," a third voice added quietly. "That's my fault."

"Who are you?" Mac asked as she jumped down and approached cautiously

"Professor Jasper Gunther. The rest doesn't matter right now. But these two are right. You need to get us out of here and you need to take care of your mom—or whoever that Jamie-person is."

Mac was about to explain who Jamie was, but decided time was being wasted. She was going to have to take her chances with these people. She returned to the front of the truck, flipped off the winch brake, and walking backwards, she dragged the heavy woven-steel cable as the winch unspooled it. When more than enough cable was on the ground, she flipped the winch from deploy to neutral. "I'm going to pass you the hook and cable through this top crack in the boards. Pass it back to me down here." She pointed to a gap between the ground and the bottom plank.

"By the way," spoke the first voice again, "my name is Eddie. I'm a rancher and a trail guide. My friend in here with me is Roland." There was a pause as he took hold of the hook and pulled the cable inside. "Here you go," he continued as the hook reappeared through the gap at the ground.

"Thanks, um . . . Eddie. My name's Mac. Mackenzie, really, but everyone just calls me Mac." She clipped the hook around the steel cable, making a loop. "Stand back, just in case something breaks or splits. I'm going to use just the winch motor first, but if that doesn't work, I'll try backing up the Cruiser." She flipped the lever to retrieve the cable and watched as the heavy-duty electric motor slowly reeled it in. As it took up the last of the slack, Mac stepped aside and watched to see which would give first, the boards or the Cruiser.

Soon she heard the eerie screech of nails slowly being pulled from wood, and thought what a great Halloween sound effect it would make. The Cruiser wasn't budging and the boards were clearly about to pry loose, so Mac quickly moved behind the truck so she wouldn't get hit by anything that might come flying. Finally, with a snap and loud crack, two of the planks were suddenly free while four others broke in half and came flying off the timbers that framed the entry. Mac was glad she'd taken cover, but was a little concerned about the Cruiser. Eric wasn't going to be too happy when he saw what one of the boards had done to his right front headlight!

The three trapped men emerged from the dark mine into the daylight, wincing at the brightness as they stepped out. "Thank you, Miss Mac, I'm Eddie," said the first as he stumbled over to where Mac was unhooking the cable from the debris. "And I'm Roland," echoed his friend. As Mac shook their hands she noticed that the one who'd identified himself as a professor was sitting on a rock by the entry, staring down at the ground.

When the cowboys spotted their horses they got excited. "Told you they'd hang around if we left 'em free," Roland bragged to Eddie as he took hold of his horse and stroked its head and shoulders.

"So, like, I'm going to need your all's help now," Mac called out to Eddie and Roland. Mac explained how Jamie was lying badly injured at the bottom of a side shaft and how she'd had to drive the Cruiser back so they could use the winch to lift her from where she had fallen.

Roland shook his head, still absorbing Mac's matter-of-fact account of getting the Cruiser up the washout. "You're telling me you took this tough old FJ40 up Widow-maker's Gulch?" He exchanged glances and raised eyebrows with Eddie and shook his head. "Girl, that's just plain crazy!"

"Well, your daddy must've *really* taught you the art of four-wheel driving if you did that all by yourself." Eddie shook his head in amazement as he flipped the winch to *deploy* to play out the cable again.

Mac grinned and paused for a moment to drink in the cowboys' astonished reactions. "My uncle Eric." she corrected

Eddie as she lugged a huge coil of climbing rope from the back end of the truck. "My uncle's the one who taught me how to drive the Cruiser. He and my dad and my cousin Tyler are down there in the mine with Jamie." She dropped the rope beside Roland. "We'll need to play out as much of this winch line as we can then attach the hook to this rope, and I'll drag it down the tunnel. Jamie may have broken her arm or her leg—or both," she said, and realized she really didn't know what kind of shape she was in.

"Yes, ma'am!" Roland said and got to work creating a loop and a knot in the end of the rope. Mac thought it looked very professional—like Roland knew exactly what he was doing. Then she put on her LED headlamp and asked Eddie to watch the feed while she headed into the mine with the cable and the rope. She told Roland to follow her about halfway, then wait so he could relay instructions back to Eddie when they were ready to winch Jamie up.

Mac began down the dark tunnel with the hook in her hand and the rope slung across a shoulder. When she was about thirty feet in, Eddie called out, "That's all of it!" She stopped and snapped the winch hook through Roland's loop and handed him the connection. Then methodically playing out the rope on the ground behind her, she moved deeper into the darkness, searching for the side passage. It seemed like it was taking forever to find it—she didn't remember it being this far down. All around her was a different kind of dark . . . and it was *very* creepy to be so deep in the black emptiness all by herself. Even if her newfound helpers were only a yell away, there was something frightening about being alone in such total darkness. It wasn't at all like those underground scenes in the movies where everything was brightly lit. In reality, *darkness is a hungry thing that eats the light.*

Finally she spotted a glow coming from the side passage ahead. "Jamie! Dad? Tyler? Eric! I'm back! Are you guys okay?"

"We're okay," he answered. "But we're sure glad you're back!" She was relieved to hear her dad's voice. "How's Jamie?"

"We're trying to keep her calm but she's in a lot of pain. Were you able to call the sheriff?"

Eric interrupted before she could answer. "Did you bring the Cruiser?"

"The sheriff's sending help and yes, I made it back with the Cruiser!" She started to tell them more when she noticed the ropes that had been attached to the rail were gone. As her headlamp scanned the main passageway she noticed something else strange—no boxes! "Where's the rope?" Mac carefully knelt and looked over the edge. She was relieved to see everyone again, but not Jamie's condition.

"We'll tell you about that later," Eric answered. "Did you see anyone on your way back?"

"Yeah, weird story. I found three guys trapped in the mine when I got here. Some boards had been nailed to the entrance. I pulled them off with the winch, and two of the guys—cowboys with real horses—are going to help us. Eddie and Roland. There's some professor guy, too. But have you-all figured out how we're going to get Jamie out?"

"We found a plank to tie her to—and we think we can rig some ropes and lift her with the winch line," her dad replied.

"Need to see if we can toss you the rope, Mac!" Eric hollered. "Whoever stole the boxes also unfastened the carabiner, and when we pulled on it, the line just came tumbling down. We've been trapped down here ever since you left." He began to circle the rope and carabiner above his head, trying to gain momentum before letting them sail up toward Mac. "Stand back, Mac!" and as soon as she moved, the rock and rope landed near her feet.

"Got it! Want me to fasten it to the rail track?"

"Yes, then we'll rig the climbing gear to work like a pulley and lift Jamie out of here. So the sheriff's on his way?"

"Yeah, but they said it was going to take a while to get here." Mac secured the carabiner and stuck her hand in the beam of light from below to give Eric a thumbs-up. "I've got one end of a 200-foot rope up here. The other is attached to the winch hook further back up the passage. Roland's there waiting for instructions, and he'll relay them to Eddie when you're ready."

"Brilliant plan!" Mac watched her dad and Tyler rig ropes around a long wide plank that would be Jamie's stretcher while Eric began his climb up the wall. Soon Eric was on the ledge giving Mac a big, long bear hug. "So proud of you, Mac!" he whispered into her ear. She thought he was going to squish her guts out before he finally released her and wiped his eyes.

"Jamie's going to be okay. But we've gotta winch her straight up. We'll attach my climbing harness to this overhead timber and its S hook will be our pulley." After removing his harness, he looped the winch-rope through the hook and tossed the rest of the line down. Using a knot his dad taught him on a campout, Tyler secured it to those already rigged to Jamie's board. It looked precarious at best but Mac was certain it would work.

"Roland!" Eric yelled up the tunnel. "I'm Eric, Mac's uncle. Can you hear me okay?"

After a moment's delay they heard, "Yes, sir, I hear you, Eric! You ready for us to start the winch?" Roland sounded like he was on the other side of the world, the way his voice echoed its way down the tunnel.

"This is very important, Roland. I just need you to take up the slack. About five feet on this first pull!"

"I hear you! A five-foot pull, then stop. Yes?"

This is the strangest way to communicate! Mac thought as she listened to Roland relay Eric's instructions to Eddie.

The rope inched along then stopped after lifting Jamie's stretcher just barely off the ground. Mac thought it looked like it was going to bang against the wall on the way up.

After Eric inspected everything he called down, "Ryan, you two ready down there?"

"Let's do this."

Mac could see that Tyler and her dad each had a rope keep the plank from bumping the wall on its way up, but it was going to be tricky.

"Roland—ten feet up and pause and wait for my command," Eric instructed, and again, Roland confirmed what he'd heard before relaying it to Eddie.

Now the plank began slowly to rise, the line pulling taut along the timber at the doorway. After the first ten feet went all right, Eric called for ten more. Jamie was now within five feet of the edge, suspended in midair and steadied by the ropes Ryan and Tyler were holding.

"Roland—I need exactly five feet!" Jamie was just inches below and within Eric's reach but this part was going to be awkward. Mac wasn't sure how he'd get her on the ledge without tipping the board sideways.

"Mac, very carefully grab ahold of those two ropes by Jamie's head. Try to get your end on the ledge when I pull down on my rope. Got it?"

"Yup." She saw exactly what Eric planned and pulled the plank onto the ledge at the same time that Eric added all his weight and got Jamie safely to the top. Eric broke out in a big smile, took his weight off the rope, and gave Mac a powerful high-five. "Want a ride up the elevator?" he called to Ryan and Tyler.

As much as Tyler thought it would be exciting, he knew it would take lots of calling back and forth between the people handling the winch, so he decided to climb up as did Ryan. Tyler sent the ropes and the rest of the equipment up then he and Ryan scaled the wall, reaching the top, both were out of breath after the twenty-five-foot rope climb.

After Eric and Ryan agreed that winching the board along the rail track would be the easiest way to get Jamie out, Ryan headed up the tunnel to explain the plan to Roland and Eddie. While they got Jamie's stretcher ready for the pull, she opened her eyes and smiled groggily at Mac. "Thank you," she murmured. "I knew you could do it." Then her eyes closed and she fell unconscious again.

40

SOMETIMES, HELP IS LATE—BUT HELP IS ALWAYS WELCOME

J amie had just been carried out from the mine on her makeshift stretcher when they heard the helicopter overhead. Eric had just figured out that the skinny professor dude was the sneaky stalker who'd followed them into the mine, caused Jamie's accident, and left them stranded. He'd just about punched him in the nose, but Eddie and Roland saw it coming and intervened. Now everyone's attention immediately focused on the chopper.

As a former Army helicopter pilot, Eric looked around and decided the clearing was large enough to land a bird like the one above. The dust being kicked up reminded him of many landings he'd made in Afghanistan. After instructing everyone to move close to the entrance of the mine, he stepped into the clearing and using aviation hand signals confirmed to the pilot that the space was secure for landing. He was confused that the helicopter wasn't medical, though. Then when the door slid open, he recognized the FBI agents he and Ryan had worked with earlier this summer. Agents Harper and Ramirez were equally surprised to see them, and pleased to see that Eddie and Roland were already free, along with the third man who turned out to be the missing professor.

After a quick debriefing from both Eddie and Eric, Harper immediately took the professor into custody for questioning. Seeing Jamie's condition, he understood why the medical helicopter was inbound. The pilot of the FBI chopper was able to patch Eric through to the air ambulance and found they were less than three minutes out and waiting for clearance to proceed to the scene. Harper instructed the pilot to take him and the professor back to the base camp, while Ramirez agreed it would be best that he remain with the family. With Harper's permission the pilot powered up the blades and lifted off, creating a second dust storm that was duplicated just minutes later by the medivac.

The EMTs quickly examined Jamie and complimented Eric on his first aid response, then established a drip line to hydrate her and began an antibiotic. Finally they put inflatable splints on her leg and arm and a brace on her neck in case of an undiagnosed injury. When she was stabilized, the crew loaded her on the chopper.

"She looks a lot worse now than when we first got her out," Tyler murmured, shaking his head.

"Absolutely" was all Mac could say. She didn't want to cry, but tears were suddenly welling up that she couldn't control.

Tyler put his arm around her shoulder and gave her a hug. "Hey, don't hold it in . . . more room on the outside than inside."

Mac looked at him quizzically. "Funny, that's what my dad says."

"Really? That's what Grandma Ruth used to say."

"Probably where it came from, right?" She smiled and blinked loose a couple of tears, then wiped her eyes with the sleeve of her shirt.

As Tyler surveyed the clearing, he noticed Eric's Land Cruiser with the winch line still strung out toward the mine. "Pretty amazing you got the Cruiser up here. No way I coulda done that!"

"But you got to fly and land a plane, and now, all my girlfriends can talk about is what a hero you are and how cool you are. They totally get landing a plane—driving a four-wheel drive truck up a gully . . . it's just not the same. That's going to go right over their heads."

"Maybe." He shook his head at the mess Mac had made of her face when she wiped away her tears with her dust-covered sleeve. "I think the guys will think it's pretty amazing though— that's gotta count for something. Anyway, your face looks like you've been in a zombie movie. Let's go see if one of those medical people can get you cleaned up."

"Great!? Now I'm a zombie heroine."

"Yeah, but not for long. Come on."

After Mac got cleaned up, she and Tyler decided to hang out on a couple of boulders and watch all the activity, which was like swarming ants once the sheriff's department arrived in their 4WD pickup. Agent Ramirez and the sheriff along with two deputies talked through the logistics of the scene, the alleged crimes, and who had what aspects of jurisdiction. They agreed that Eric could leave with Jamie in the medical helicopter while they took statements from the others.

Eric walked over to the two kids and gave them an update. "So at this point, it looks like everybody's going to get interviewed by the deputies, then you two and Ryan will take the Cruiser home. In the meantime, best way you can help is get all the ropes and gear back in the Cruiser and rewind the winch. We'll come back later to get the four-wheelers. Use some of the logging chain to secure this quad. We'll deal with the one back at the draw and the rest of this later."

An EMT came over to let Eric know it was time to leave. "Catch up with you after I know more about Jamie." He started to turn but instead paused and shook his head as he looked Mac in the eyes. "You're awesome, Mackenzie. You did us proud, today." He held out his hand for a high-five, then turned and trotted behind the EMT to climb into the waiting helicopter.

Mac blushed and started to tear up, but before she could use her dirty tee shirt again, Tyler intervened: "Stop with the zombie effect already! Lemme grab you something from the Cruiser to wipe your face, okay?" which made her laugh. It was one of those deep laughs that cleaned out all the tension that had built up this afternoon and caught Tyler off guard but before he knew it he was laughing, too.

Mac and Tyler loaded up the Cruiser while Ryan spoke with the deputies. After that, it was Eddie and Roland's turn. When Ramirez agreed they were done, they and their horses headed back to join David and Matt. Then Ramirez and the deputies interviewed Mac and Tyler separately, and finally, all the details had been completed to the sheriff's satisfaction.

In spite of loose ends like the quad runners, questions about who the professor guy was, and the huge question of what was going to happen to the boxes they'd found, they were finished at the mine. Ryan agreed to follow the sheriff back down the canyon trail in Eric's Cruiser. There'd be plenty of time to sort out other details and unanswered questions later.

41
TIME TO TALK

Ryan had been following the two-lane farm-to-market road ever since leaving the canyon and now turned to accelerate down the entrance ramp and onto westbound Interstate 10. Mac blinked at the sun, now low in the western sky and found it suddenly annoying the way it drew her concentration away from replaying the collapse that had led to Jamie's fall. The ride had been quiet, and the silence had given her brain a chance to cycle through everything that had happened, especially the terror of the collapse. Before that was the hill climb and the rattlesnake . . . she couldn't decide yet which was the most frightening of the three. But now, seeing cars and trucks passing them on the interstate brought a strange sense of relief—which felt curious itself. Then it dawned on her that from the moment she'd left the mine facing the impossible task of driving the Cruiser back up, she'd felt alone and isolated.

"You're being awfully noisy over there."

Mac looked at her dad and sort of smiled, still not sure what to make of the day. "Sorry. Just kinda spaced out over here."

"You haven't really said much about what you did up there today, but I sure was glad to hear your voice from up on top that scaffolding when you got back."

"Thanks." Mac turned to look out the window again, spellbound by the endless desert landscape. "Still pretty bizarre to think about all of it."

"Absolutely agree." He looked over his shoulder and then changed lanes to pass an old, slow moving blue pickup piled high with scrap metal. "And pretty amazing you were able to get up that hill." He glanced toward Mac again. "Wanna tell me about it?"

Mac looked at her dad and noticed that Tyler was anxious to hear the story, too. She began with the call to the sheriff, then how she'd looked down the draw from the top and planned her route up, and then the rattlesnake . . .

"Rattlesnake?!" Tyler perked up at that point. "You saw a rattlesnake?"

"Un huh. I almost stepped in front of it—one more step and I woulda been a goner!"

"How big was it?" To Tyler, encountering a rattlesnake sounded both frightening and exciting at the same time.

"Probably about six feet long and as fat as your wrist."

"Yeesh! What'd you do?"

Mac described how she'd slowly backed up and honked the ATV horn. And then after the snake wriggled away under the truck, how she had to decide if it was safe to run and jump into the Cruiser.

"And you did all this *before* the hill climb?" Her dad was in awe.

"Yeah. Just a minor heart attack in a crazy day, right?" She found herself laughing at herself and that made her suddenly feel more comfortable. "So after I recovered from that and was ready to get underway . . . I managed to kill the motor two or three times. Then I remembered about the transfer case." She went on to describe the climb, the gates, the challenges, almost not making it up, and then freaking out about driving along the skinny trail once she'd made it to the top.

"Dang! That's amazing!" Tyler exclaimed when she finished. He relaxed and leaned back in his seat again. "Ethan and Benji are going to be totally wowed!"

"You know, your mom's going to be very proud of what you did up there today, Mac. Heck, *I'm* proud of you!" Ryan shook his head in amazement as he focused on the road. "No, seriously. Very proud of you. I'm still not sure how you did it— even after hearing you tell it."

"Yeah, you'll be telling that story to your grandkids when you're an old lady!" Tyler teased as he gave her seat back a playful push.

Mac again looked out her window at the desert and the sharp outline of the mountains where they'd spent the day. *Maybe I really am the hero I'd like to be. Who knows? Maybe my friends will think so too.* She stole a glance back at Tyler without him noticing. *Yeah, and maybe Tyler and I are even-up—at least for this afternoon!*

42

HOSPITAL

"I just caught Dr. Waters out by the nurses' station," Eric was trying to open the door to Jamie's room while juggling a sandwich and drink from the hospital cafeteria. "She said the report she got back this morning shows everything's looking good and they might send you over to the rehab unit tomorrow!"

"Great—I guess . . ." Jamie's arm was in a cast that was suspended from a hoist on one side of the bed; her leg, which was in a cast up to her thigh, was in a harness on the other. It had been six days now since the accident and the worst of the pain was behind her. Well, except for her ribs. They still hurt when she laughed or took a deep breath.

"At least you're starting to look like you feel *some* better." He could sense the uncertainty in Jamie's response to his news.

"The swelling and bruising have pretty much faded, you know."

"Thanks, I think," she replied, forcing a small smile. She knew Eric was trying hard to help her feel better, but six days was a long time to be in a bed with your arm and leg in suspension casts. The prospect of several more weeks like this sounded like forever right now.

A light rapping of knuckles on her door was followed by a familiar face peeking in. "You okay with some company?" Becky stepped in, followed by Ryan, Mackenzie, and Tyler.

"Feeling any better today?" Ryan asked as he moved to the window side of the bed to make more room.

"Some better." But she didn't sound very convincing. "Eric was talking to the doctor and she said they might move me to rehab tomorrow."

"That sounds like good progress!" Becky leaned over and brushed a piece of stray hair from Jamie's forehead.

"We brought you some sunflowers." Mac held up the blue glass vase for Jamie to get a good look before setting them on the window ledge.

"They're beautiful," Jamie turned her head to study the bouquet.

"We figured your yellow roses were about ready to bite the dust!" Tyler looked around for the flowers they'd brought earlier in the week.

"They're gone already. Eric asked the nurse to toss them this morning. Perfect timing for fresh ones!"

Tyler examined the harnesses holding up Jamie's two casts, then looked closer at her face. "That big raspberry you had on your nose and cheek has just about disappeared," he reported to her encouragingly.

Jamie nodded. "Yeah. The nurses have me putting some special cream on it several times a day—something with a lot of aloe and vitamin E in it. Supposed to prevent scars on your face." With her good hand she carefully touched the place that had looked so battered and bruised when she was pulled from the mine.

In the meantime, Eric had moved over next to Ryan. "That Agent Ramirez with the FBI called me this morning. Told me he'd drop by this afternoon with an update on the case."

"That'd be nice. It sounded like he was just about wrapped up with his investigation last week, but I'd sure like to know where things stand."

Eric took another bite of his sandwich and offered Ryan and Tyler some of his chips.

Ryan politely declined, then asked, "By the way, what about your flight time? Have you and Clayton been able to get back to your full schedule?"

"Clayton had us booked at about sixty-five hours this week, so yeah, I think we're pretty much back." He glanced over at Jamie, who was still visiting with Becky and Mac. "I had an early morning flight this morning, and a break this afternoon, so I decided to spend some extra time with Jamie." Eric finished his sandwich, crumpled the paper, and tossed it in a perfect arc across the room into the trash can.

"I'll give you three points for that one," Tyler said, impressed.

There was another knock on Jamie's door. "Come in," she responded softly and Agent Ramirez entered with a tan leather portfolio. He greeted everyone by their first name before moving over to say hi to Jamie.

"You look like you've made quite a bit of progress since I saw you last!"

"I'm told they are about to evict me and send me to rehab," she replied with a smile.

Ryan, anxious for news about the case interrupted the small

talk. "Eric says you've got an update for us this afternoon."

"I do, actually," Ramirez acknowledged, nodding his head. He looked around and decided to sit on the arm of the sofa below the window. It was a perfect perch for speaking to the group, and more importantly, he wouldn't have his back to the door—a professional detail he was always careful to observe.

"Did you ever figure out what was going on with that Jasper Gunther guy? Was he really a professor?" Eric asked.

"And is he the one who stole the photo from my gallery show?" Jamie managed to ask.

"Yes, and yes." Ramirez smiled at the enthusiasm of this family—he liked them and their easygoing but determined approach to life. "We've been talking with Professor Gunther over the past week—he's been very forthcoming on behalf of our investigation. You'll understand that much of his statement has to be kept confidential, based on a potential presentation to a federal grand jury . . ."

"I get it," Eric interrupted, holding up his hand. "Yes, he's been a help, but no, you can't tell us anything right now, right?"

"No, there's definitely some info I can tell you. All of you have already provided a statement, so I've got *some* information that might clarify a few of the events. In particular, Professor Gunther made some admissions in a hearing earlier this week as part of a plea bargain agreement, so I think I can clear up some of the mystery for you."

"Well, then," Becky said with a twinkle in her eye. "Do tell!" She was enjoying this bit of inside drama.

"Let's start with why he was at the mine in the first place," Ramirez began. "The original Gunther that the mine was jointly named for was Professor Gunther's great-grandfather. When the professor's dad passed away last year, he left him all of his grandfather's papers and books. Gunther's a geologist and a junior professor at the university, and when he found the map and notebooks he'd been shown when he was a child, he was convinced—as a geologist—that there was a geologic phenomenon called a parallel vein at the site. He was felt certain, in spite of the mine having already been worked, there would be a second find almost as big as the first, just waiting to be located."

"So he wasn't looking for the treasure?" Tyler asked.

"No. He was after that second vein. He spent two weeks and quite a lot of money, exploring and doing his own survey work to test his theory. He borrowed the money for the initial exploration, but he still hadn't found any evidence to back up his assumption when the cash ran out. That was when he got ready to head back to El Paso and a reckoning with a local loan shark who had underwritten Gunther's unproven bet." Ramirez paused.

"The loans tie into another case we were already working on, but that's really not what started *your* involvement with him." He glanced toward Eric. "Nope, none of this story would ever have involved you all, except that on his way home from the mine, he got his little Subaru stuck. High-centered it trying to cross a washout not far from the mine."

"And I bet I know exactly where!" Mac said triumphantly, remembering the rough spot they'd carefully crossed on their way down the side trail to the mine.

Ramirez nodded. "Yup. So Gunther had to hike down the backside of the mountain and out across the desert toward I-10. Any guesses where he eventually ends up that afternoon?"

"My place," Eric nodded. "So he's the one who broke in with my hidden key and then stole my Kawasaki . . ."

"That's right. He's admitted to breaking and entering both your place and the trailer down the road from you, and to several related thefts." Ramirez paused to make sure everyone was with him. "His excuse was that he was fatigued, disoriented, and under duress from a loan issue gone bad."

"Right," Eric growled. He was still angry—no rationale was an adequate excuse for breaking into his ranch or for what happened to Jamie.

"Well," Ramirez continued, "whatever punishment or restitution Gunther gets will be for a judge to decide based on his plea deal."

Eric nodded. He understood that the prosecutors and a judge would have to settle all of that. It just wouldn't be easy to see Gunther get off too easy.

The look on Ramirez's face indicated the agent understood all too well the mixed emotions Eric had right now. "In any case, that's how Gunther ended up at your place. He stole your four-wheeler to get back to his car and winch it out. After that, he headed home but when he got to his street, he said he believed that the person he'd borrowed money from was looking for him."

"And since his mine was a bust he had to run away, right?" Ryan interrupted.

"Kind of. He holed up at a local motel and wandered around town that evening trying to figure out what he was going to do. That's when he stumbled onto Jamie's gallery show."

"Wait a minute." Jamie turned her head to look at Ramirez. "You're telling me that the guy who stole Eric's four-wheeler is the same one who stole my prize photo?"

"Yes, ma'am," Ramirez nodded. "One and the same."

"I don't get it. Did he say why?"

"At this point we're still not certain what was going on with him mentally. He seems to have been acting totally out of character over the course of the several days in question. Almost with a psychotic paranoia," Ramirez noted. "In any case, his story is that when he saw your photo on the wall that afternoon he immediately recognized the location. He became irrationally convinced that you were somehow giving away the secret about his mine." Ramirez shook his head. "Unfortunately, it isn't the first time in my line of work that I've seen an otherwise normal, intelligent person go off the rails like this."

"So that's why he came back to the mine?" Mackenzie asked. "He thought we were there to steal some secret about a hidden vein of silver?"

"Right again, Mac!" he smiled and gave her a subtle wink.

"The professor had only just left your trailer when you showed up last week. He was over at the next trailer—that yellow one down the road watching all of you with a pair of binoculars."

"That's too creepy!" Mac grimaced.

"Fact is, if you had looked in your neighbor's yard, you would have spotted your four-wheeler. But the point is, when he looked you up online, Jamie, and saw a picture posted of you and Eric, he recognized you as the couple he'd seen at the trailer. He also realized he'd left his map behind at your trailer. So he became convinced you were going to head to the mine at some point soon. Then when the five of you did, in fact, show up on your treasure hunt, he admits to following you in. Remember, he was very familiar with that mine and didn't need a light to find his way around."

"I'm afraid to ask what happened next, but I think I know," Jamie murmured.

"Yes. He admits collecting your yellow guide rope as he entered the mine and tossing it into a side passage where it fell into the pit." Ramirez looked at Jamie and then at Eric. "A reasonable person would have understood the consequences of what he'd done, but Professor Gunther argues that it wasn't a premeditated intent to harm but was more of an impulsive intent to obstruct your easy exit."

"Yeah, right." Eric didn't buy any of the excuses he was hearing.

"Well, he'll face state charges. Reckless endangerment at the very least."

"If nothing else, I suspect there's a good case for a civil suit against him for what happened to Jamie," Ryan added, looking over at his brother-in-law.

"And . . . there's one other thing you wouldn't have understood at the time. You were all focused on getting Jamie medical attention, right? Well, he'd overheard you earlier in the room where you found those boxes. He hadn't been aware of anything about a treasure in the mine. On the other hand, he was determined to make the most of the misfortune he'd created when Jamie followed the rope and fell. He saw it as his golden opportunity to steal the boxes and use whatever was in them to escape his financial problems."

There was a silent consideration of these new details as everybody in the room thought about what they'd just heard. Tyler finally broke the silence. "And why were you there, Agent Ramirez? Why did the FBI just happen to be in the neighborhood? I still don't get that part."

"I can't discuss that in detail, Tyler," Ramirez apologized. "All I *can* tell you is that the individual who stole the treasure from the professor and falsely imprisoned the professor and the two cowboys by boarding them inside the mine . . . and then rode away on your ATV with the two boxes, well, he was already under surveillance as a person of interest."

Mac suddenly remembered something. "So I'll bet that was *your* drone I saw when I was in the Cruiser! The one that exploded in a million pieces . . ." Mac looked intently at Agent Ramirez.

"Drone? What drone?" Ramirez smiled as he tilted his head to emphasize his mock question. "Are you certain you saw a drone?"

Mac started to protest and then realized Agent Ramirez couldn't admit to anything about the drone just now. "Okay, I get it. But, yes, I did see a drone," she grinned.

"Well, I think that just about covers everything I can tell you for now." The agent looked around the room at each of them.

"What about the boxes?" Tyler asked. "When do we get them back?"

"Good question, Tyler. Right now they're in our evidence facility pending a legal review. Our legal team is going to have to do some research before they can release them. But since they were lashed down to Eric's stolen ATV at the time they were recovered, we'll be in touch with Eric when a decision has been made on what happens to them."

"The evidence guys have already gotten back with me about the stolen ATV," Eric added. "Pretty banged up, but my insurance company plans to repair it. And they also let me know they'd found my Kawasaki hidden in some brush up near the mine. I got that back a couple of days ago."

"Great! Stolen property is typically gone forever. Glad you were the exception." Ramirez stood to leave, but first he went over to Jamie. "I'm so sorry that this happened to you, Ms. Smythe, but thank goodness there were resources to get you medical attention so quickly. I've been told you're on track to make a good recovery. I'll continue to be in touch." He carefully squeezed her good hand then stepped over to where Mac was standing, "By the way, Mackenzie, congratulations on a job well done! I've read the statements and the After Incident reports and have to say I am very, *very* impressed at your contribution to Ms. Smythe's rescue." He gave her a fist bump and a wink then said goodbye to everyone.

After Agent Ramirez had left, and the pride of the moment had receded, it was Mac who asked the question that was on the top of everyone's mind . . . the elephant-in-the-corner-of-the-room question:

"So what do you think is going to happen to the treasure now?"

43

THE FORT HANCOCK PAYROLL ROBBERY OF 1902 - EPILOGUE

B ecky looked over the letter and its envelope once more. It offered very few details, but it was an invitation and had been sent on the formal stationery of the law firm Maguire, Cavan, Schull & Bantry. The fancy business envelope matched the letter's cream-colored paper. Even after reading it twice, Becky thought it sounded intimidating.

To: Mr. Ryan Foster and Mr. Eric Wilson on the behalf of named individuals: Jamie Smythe; Mackenzie Foster (a minor); Tyler Dubois (a minor),

On behalf of: Ms. Sandra Morrison-Parker

By this letter, please be advised of Ms. Morrison-Parker's invitation to meet with you in our offices on the 23rd floor of the Pace Setter Bank Tower in downtown El Paso at 10:30 a.m. on Wednesday, July 19.

Ms. Morrison-Parker has matters she would like to discuss related to recent events at the Gunther-Morrison Mine Property [AKA "Property 89-017"] which is a wholly owned holding of the Morrison Family Trust.

July 19 is a preferred date based on Ms. Morrison-Parker's personal calendar. If, however, you are unavailable at this date and time, please advise my clerk Mr. D. Johnston and a more satisfactory appointment can be arranged.

With kindest regards,
Travis Maguire, Sr. Partner

She handed the letter back to Ryan. "I guess we should've thought through that little outing a bit more." She shook her head. "Between Jamie's fall, a run-in with a very bad dude, a close encounter with the FBI, and Mac having to drive Eric's Land Cruiser . . . well, I'm pretty certain it was not our shining moment as parents." Becky shook her head once more.

"It was an abandoned mine up in the mountains that hadn't been worked since the late 1800s." Ryan set the letter on the table. "Looking back now, of course, it's perfectly obvious that someone *had* to have owned the property. It just didn't occur to me at the time."

"So to be blunt, our little harebrained idea to explore it was, in fact, a trespass on private property, right?" Becky already knew the answer.

"No question. Stupid idea in hindsight." Ryan frowned, then looked at his wife. "So what do you think this woman, this Ms. Parker-Morrison, wants to discuss?"

"I'm sure she wants to talk about what she's going to do with those boxes. Hopefully she's not thinking about bringing trespass charges. But if she was going to do that, I don't think you'd get a formal invitation on fancy stationery."

"You're probably right." Ryan glanced at the letter once more, then folded it and put it back in its envelope. "Guess I'll just need to take the morning off work next week and find out."

"Are you going to take everyone with you?" Becky was trying to imagine the conference room of a downtown law firm with her husband and Eric, plus Jamie in her two casts, along with Tyler and Mac—all around a giant mahogany table. And across from them, some woman named Sandra Morrison-Parker and her attorney.

"I suspect it would be best if we were all there. Safety in numbers in an unfamiliar situation—right?"

"Pretty much. Better talk to the kids about this when they get back from your mom's house tomorrow. I'll give Eric a call in a few minutes to see if he's seen his copy of it."

# # #

On Wednesday Ryan and the kids rode the glass elevator to the twenty-third floor of the Rio National Bank Tower accompanied by Eric pushing Jamie in her wheelchair. She felt embarrassed to be wheeled around, but at least she was finally out of the hospital and in a more comfortable leg cast. Most important, she was mobile. Sort of.

They arrived fifteen minutes early and were warmly welcomed by Mr. Maguire's clerk, who introduced himself as

Daniel Johnston and then escorted them to a large conference room with floor-to-ceiling glass walls. Mac and Tyler were excited to visit a downtown office tower for the first time and were impressed with the cool view of El Paso from the twenty-third floor. They picked chairs facing the big window.

Johnston brought a tray of water and soft drinks and a carafe of coffee, setting it on the credenza, before stepping out and leaving them alone. While Jamie pointed out that the glasses were crystal and the coffee cups and saucers were fine china, Ryan reminded Mac and Tyler of their discussion in the car to let him and Eric do the talking. They could speak if specifically addressed, but until they all understood where this was going, the less said the better.

The door opened again, and Johnston waited respectfully as a well-dressed woman wearing a classic string of pearls stepped into the room. Eric guessed she might be seventy years old, but she had a commanding presence that made her age immediately irrelevant. A very tall man with beautiful white hair and distinguished features strode in behind her. He was dressed in a fine gray suit, which, Ryan presumed, had likely been custom-made in Italy, with a crisp white shirt and a formal blue necktie that was likely silk. Ryan guessed this was the senior legal partner, Mr. Maguire.

Ms. Morrison-Parker extended her hand to Eric, who was standing closest to her, and then to Jamie as she introduced herself. She offered her condolences to Jamie on the injuries and asked how she was recovering. She then shook hands with Ryan and moved behind the chairs to also greet Mackenzie and Tyler. She struck Tyler as very pleasant and reminded him a little bit of his dad's mom. He hadn't spent a lot of time with his Nana Dubois over the years, but he thought they were both a lot alike: confident women with big friendly smiles and amazing

240

green eyes. And they both wore pearls.

Mac liked the way the lady greeted each of them personally and was intrigued by her almost perfect smile and teeth. She looked pretty impressive for somebody who must be at least as old as her grandma Foster.

Jamie thought Ms. Morrison-Parker's lemon yellow jacket and skirt suit was very sharp, and the pearls were a simple yet elegant touch. The shoes, which perfectly matched her suit, had short sensible heels. Something a person could walk in. Her hair was short and well-styled.

After they were seated and Johnston had poured a cup of black coffee for Ms. Morrison-Parker, Maguire looked around the table and opened the meeting. "Thank you all for coming today. My client, Ms. Morrison-Parker, asked me to invite you here. . ."

"Travis," she interrupted, touching her attorney's hand to pause him, "if you don't mind, I think that sounds like such a mouthful, don't you?" She caught the eyes of each of them as she continued. "Please, call me Sandra. It's so much easier." She turned again to her attorney and withdrew her hand so he could continue.

Maguire nodded. "Certainly, Sandra, as you wish. Sandra is the chair of the Morrison-Parker family trust. She asked that I invite you to visit with her today so that we might get to know each other. And more specifically, she asked that—how can I say this? See if we might *clear up* a few details with regard to the incident at the mine owned by her family's trust." He looked at Sandra, who nodded her approval. "I believe you are all familiar with that matter."

Eric nodded as Ryan replied for all of them. "Of course." He wasn't flustered by the attorney or overawed by his polite demeanor. He could, however, sense that Maguire was a formidable force. He wouldn't want to tangle with him in a courtroom. "While we're making introductions, may I just make a quick comment to Ms. Morrison? . . . I mean, Sandra."

Maguire nodded, glanced at his client, and leaned back in his chair.

"On behalf of myself, my brother-in-law Eric, his fiancée Jamie, and Mac and Tyler . . . well, let me admit how foolish Eric and I feel about all of this." He smiled and made eye contact with Sandra. "What started out as an adventurous outing with the kids, well, unfortunately it turned into a difficult and dangerous afternoon." He paused and glanced at Jamie, Mac, and Tyler before meeting Sandra's eyes again. "Frankly, in our excitement and haste, the idea of trying to locate the current owner of the property didn't come up. We knew from our research that the mine operations had ended in the late 1890s, and we thought of the site the same way you might consider poking around an old ghost town."

"It does, however, strike me as a very dangerous outing, does it not?" Maguire's voice showed real concern.

"Yes sir, it does," Eric replied before his brother-in-law could answer. "But let's be frank. I'm a former helicopter pilot and Army Ranger with multiple tours in Afghanistan. I'm a sportsman, a rock climber, and I have a ranch less than ten miles from the mine. You could say I'm familiar with the area."

He glanced at Ryan. "And so, yes, Ryan is right. We blew through the permission thing. Big mistake. But there was no error in our preparation. We were well prepared for what we undertook." Eric spoke with the firm but polite confidence that came from his years in the military. No one interrupted.

"After our discussions with the FBI, we now know that Jamie's injuries were the direct result of a deliberate act of sabotage by a man who'd been surveying your mine in hopes of discovering a lost vein of silver ore." Eric was determined to emphasize that Jamie didn't get hurt because they'd been careless. "So with all due respect, we were not poorly prepared nor could we be considered any more careless than parents who take their kids rock climbing or desert hiking or shooting rapids." He ended with a smile and waited for a rebuttal or rebuke from the lawyer. Instead it was Sandra who spoke.

"Friends, inviting you here today was not meant to be an investigation or an inquisition." She turned to make certain her attorney was going to follow her lead. "I have to say that I asked for this meeting precisely because I was so very impressed by what you did and what I heard about you all. And by the way, I followed the story earlier this summer about Tyler, here, piloting that airplane. I recall that, Eric, you were unable to fly and Tyler, you flew the plane successfully back to El Paso from the old Marfa Airbase. Is that right?"

"Yes ma'am," Tyler nodded and smiled.

"I can't say how excited I am to meet each of you today! I'm anxious to hear what led you to such a remarkable discovery in our old family mine. After all, those four boxes have been hidden for over 115 years!"

Eric and Ryan were relieved, and Jamie too, but she was watching Maguire, who didn't seem to completely share his client's enthusiasm. After a moment, however, he relaxed and leaned in to provide a comment. "Sandra is right. Naturally I'm concerned with trespass, injury, and legal matters. But she and I have discussed this, and to be upfront with you, there is to be no pursuit of any civil or criminal charges with respect to your activities, per Sandra's explicit wishes in this matter."

"Thank you, Travis." Sandra smiled. "Now—I so want to hear your story firsthand. Who would like to begin? I'm all ears and I *love* a good adventure!"

Ryan turned to Jamie. "Jamie and the kids can tell you why we believed that loot from the Ft. Hancock robbery was hidden in the mine. I'll let Eric tell you about the visit to the mine itself."

"Perfect! I used to read Nancy Drew novels as a young girl—this sounds just like such a grand adventure story!" With a huge smile on her face and the fascination of a young child, she leaned back in her chair and faced Jamie.

For the next twenty minutes, Sandra heard a full, first-hand account—which clearly delighted her. When the story was complete and all questions had been asked and answered, Ryan glanced at his watch and apologized for taking so much time, but Sandra ignored his concern.

"That is simply the most thrilling, real-life story I have ever heard!" she marveled, applauding in appreciation. "Have you ever heard anything so exciting, Travis?"

"Well, it certainly ranks right up there, Sandra."

"Mac, we must have lunch next week and talk. That is, if your parents don't object." Sandra looked at Ryan, who nodded his approval. "And Jamie, I'd like to invite you along as well. I'm eager to get to know both of you. And I have a project I'd like to discuss." She then leaned forward, rested her hands on the table, and took control of the meeting again. Ryan noticed that at this cue, Maguire pulled a legal file folder from his stack of files and papers and passed it to her. *Now what?* he asked himself.

"Having heard that terrific story, now is the perfect time to share some exciting news with all of you," Sandra began. "Travis has been working on the legal issues that a situation like this raises: stolen and buried treasure found on private property via trespass." She smiled and winked at Mac. "As you correctly guessed from your young friend's research, those four boxes did indeed come from the 1902 Fort Hancock payroll robbery."

"We never had a chance to see what was in them," Ryan

interrupted. "I assume they were silver dollars."

"They certainly were, Ryan," Sandra nodded. "The FBI determined that the contents of the boxes should be returned to our family trust as owners of the property upon which the boxes had been recovered. And let me add, that based on what you told the FBI, we paid a team of professionals to return to the mine site and collect the other two boxes." She looked at her papers and read them some facts about the treasure. "All told, the stolen 1902 payroll amounted to $6,000 at the time, made up of 6,000 uncirculated Morgan silver dollars. With 1,500 coins inside each box, those boxes weighed over 90 pounds apiece!"

"No wonder they were so heavy!" Tyler exclaimed, and everyone at the table laughed. "But $6,000 doesn't sound like a lot of money for all that weight, does it?"

"Well, Tyler," Maguire responded, "what $6,000 could buy in 1902 would cost more than $170,000 to purchase today."

Mac and Tyler were astounded.

"I did some additional research," Maguire continued. "Did you know that the average worker made only about $350 a *year* in the early part of the 1900s? In that context a $6000 robbery was a very big deal."

"In any case," Sandra added, "what you found is going to be worth a great deal, and not just because of inflation. The real value is in the *type* of coins in the boxes."

Maguire pulled a folder from his stack and passed around several color photographs. The first showed an open box with three cloth bags of coins inside. Another was a close-up of the lettering and mint information printed on each bag, and the final two were enlarged, high-resolution photos of the front and the back of a single coin.

"Prior to this assignment, I knew very little about rare coins." Maguire had become more serious. "I was aware that uncirculated coins were worth more than circulated, and that some US Mint markings are more valuable than others because they're more rare. Do you see this little mark here?" He pointed to the S in a close-up of a coin with his yellow pencil. "In this case, these 6,000 coins are uncirculated 1902 Morgan silver dollars that were minted in San Francisco. They are very rare and highly sought-after by collectors.

"Your find, ironically, may actually cause the value of an uncirculated 1902 San Francisco silver dollar to eventually drop a bit, simply due to the number of coins you found. But even allowing for that, the value of your discovery has been initially estimated at between 1.2 and 1.8 million dollars."

Tyler turned to Mac. "Totally amazing."

Mac simply nodded in reply, her eyes wide in surprise and awe.

44
BUT WAIT . . .
THERE'S MORE!

R yan looked over to Sandra, wondering what she was up to and why she and her attorney were sharing this much information with them. She caught his eye and winked, acknowledging that she understood his curiosity about the true reason for this meeting.

"Travis has carefully researched the legal ownership of a stolen treasure of this sort," she continued. "Things like treasure can be kind of tricky but in short, let him tell you what he's found out."

The attorney began a detailed explanation. "The insurers of the Matthew Brothers Cartage & Stage Line at the time of the robbery was a company called the Pecos & Santa Fe Insurance Bureau." He looked up from his notes then continued. "The payroll arrived from San Francisco by rail. Matthew Brothers picked up the shipment at the army depot in El Paso as hired, and set out to deliver the coins to Fort Hancock. But before reaching the fort they were ambushed and four payroll boxes were stolen. After the robbery, the stage line was obligated by their contract with the army to make good on any loss suffered, regardless of cause or fault. So their insurance company—Pecos & Santa Fe—covered 90 percent of the theft and the stage line came up with the difference. That means the army has no outstanding claim on the treasure because their loss was made good. With me so far?"

They all nodded and he continued. "A short time later, Pecos & Santa Fe published their notice of a reward for recovery: $500 cash plus a 25 percent share of whatever loss was recovered." He looked up from his paper. "That was a fairly typical 'bounty-plus' recovery offer in that day," he said as an aside.

Eric smiled. "I'm in the air cargo business and we have similar terms still today. My policy requires me to cover the first 15 percent of a loss, then they'll pay the client's claim and get the recovery rights to any and all recovery. Pretty much the same deal."

"Exactly. So if Pecos & Santa Fe were still in business today, or if they'd been absorbed into some successor company, they would be legally entitled to make a claim against the value of the treasure even this many years later."

"But . . . ?" Eric asked, expecting some big reveal.

"But Pecos & Santa Fe ceased all operations in 1915," Sandra interrupted. "Apparently they were bankrupted by insured claims against them following the sinking of the *Lusitania* near the start of World War I. And although there could have been claims at that point by creditors that otherwise could have survived, there is also a statute of limitations for bankruptcy claims."

"I think you're about to say that there are no competing

claims on this find." Eric's voice was a mix of curiosity and excitement.

Maguire nodded. "There is no statutory basis of claim by Pecos & Santa Fe nor any successor nor any bankruptcy claimant. As a result, this treasure passes into a status known as 'rights of ownership for mislaid property.'"

"So," Ryan concluded, "even though these boxes were originally stolen property, your family trust now has full legal title to the silver in those boxes. Right?"

"That's correct. Our lack of prior knowledge as to the existence of this treasure on our property doesn't change its status as mislaid property. The family trust does, indeed, own it in full."

"Well, I'm not surprised," Ryan said with a hint of disappointment in his voice. "I'm no lawyer, but we suspected that would be the case." He looked at Mac, Tyler, Eric, and Jamie. "But, as you can imagine, it's kind of disappointing all the same."

"I certainly do understand that disappointment!" Sandra was quick to reassure him and looked very serious. "I didn't invite you all here today just to shower you with legalese. Not at all!" And then her eyes began to twinkle like a kid about to open a present. "You will recall that the Pecos & Santa Fe Insurance Company had offered a reward in 1902 of $500 plus 25 percent of the recovery to anyone who could deliver the stolen property. Well, I'm told an appropriate finder's fee is almost always paid in this type of recovery, even today!"

Sandra passed a copy of a legal document to each of them. Then she began to read from her notes: "The current value of a $500 reward posted in 1902 would be a bit over $14,500 today. Therefore, I've instructed Mr. Maguire, on behalf of the Morrison Family Trust, to offer the five of you a joint reward of $15,000 plus 25 percent of the gross value we receive for the coins when they come to auction."

Eric looked at Jamie, Mac looked at Tyler, Ryan looked at all of them, and then at Sandra. "That's extremely generous," Ryan finally responded, speaking for the group, who all sat in stunned silence ". . . and thank you!"

Suddenly, Mac blurted out, "But what about Alex? He's the one who really figured this all out!"

"Mac's right," Tyler added. "And what about Aunt Becky? She knew about Shakespeare and all that stuff, and that's what got Alex connecting the dots on the cypher, right?"

Jamie nodded. "They have a point," Eric said to Ryan. "They may not have been in the mine with us, but if the Morrison Trust is going to make a group reward, I think it should be a seven-way split, not five."

Jamie turned to Sandra. "This is incredibly generous . . . it's amazing, really! But Mac and Tyler are right about Becky and Alex. Would you object to arranging your reward to be split seven ways instead of five?"

"I see no problem with that, do you, Travis?"

"We can divide it anyway you like, Sandra." He was smiling at the generosity of the group. It was both surprising and refreshing to see.

While everyone was talking, Tyler borrowed Mac's cell phone to do some math. A seven-way split was 14.29 percent apiece. So that meant the split on the $15,000 reward would work out to a little over two thousand dollars apiece. Sweet! He ran another calculation. If the silver really was worth a minimum of $1.2 million then it meant they'd split another $300,000 seven ways . . . *about $43,000 each!*

He looked out the window and thought about his dad over in Singapore and their FaceTime and Skype calls two or three times a week. He was *never* going to believe what happened today. As he turned back around, everyone was shaking hands and smiling and suddenly Tyler realized something was missing: a photo.

A few minutes later Maguire returned with Johnston who used Mac's cell phone to take a picture of the group with Sandra.

What a summer!

45

WHAT A SUMMER, INDEED!

On a sunny Saturday afternoon, a cookout was underway in the backyard of the Morrison-Parker estate on the outskirts of El Paso. The sprawling home had been designed in the traditional Spanish-colonial style of haciendas built in Colonial Mexico and throughout the upper Rio Grande Valley.

Looking up from his plate of enchiladas and beans, Tyler tried to take a rough count of the guests around the pool and under the generous shade porches of the balconies and arbors. He came up with about fifty-five—and that was just the guests outside. He figured there were another twenty touring the rooms inside the hacienda.

"Cool house!" Mac joined him and studied the house too, appreciating the details her dad had pointed out to her earlier. "Dad always likes telling me about a building's architecture, and I think he's in love with this place."

"Super impressive, isn't it. What's not to love?"

Alex arrived with his second plate of soft corn tacos and sat down. "My mom thinks this place is pretty amazing!" He took a big bite of a well-stuffed taco. "I think it's a great place for a party, too. Just wish all our friends were here and we could try out her pool!"

"Not sure I'd be much into swimming with all of these important people around." Tyler nodded toward Sandra and a tall woman near the double glass doors into the hacienda. "See that person she's talking with? That's the mayor! She introduced me to her a few minutes ago."

"Whoa . . ." Alex was suitably impressed, then took another bite of his taco.

"Are we still supposed to call her Sandra, even at this party?" Mac looked around and spotted another face she knew. "Look, she even invited our school principal, Miss Adams. There she is, over there." Mac nodded toward a group of adults near the pool cabana.

"My mom said this is going to be a great opportunity for her to make some contacts that she can follow up with later," Alex said. "You know, business and that stuff."

It wasn't long before Sandra moved to the center of the patio and started tinking a spoon on a glass to get everyone's attention. "Friends . . ." she spoke loudly, trying to interrupt the dozen or more conversations around the pool. "Friends, I appreciate everyone coming this afternoon to pay special recognition to a team of modern day, local adventurers! Will you join me in recognizing our bold guests of honor this afternoon: Mackenzie

Foster, Tyler Dubois, Alex Ortiz, Becky and Ryan Foster, Eric Wilson, and Jamie Smythe!" She set down her glass and raised her hands. "Let's give it up for this amazing puzzle-solving team!" Everyone in the courtyard joined her in applause and the few who were still inside made their way outside to join in.

Sandra pointed to each of the group then waved Mac, Tyler, and Alex over to join her. "This group has an exciting story you'll want to read; they deciphered an old treasure map and dared the dangerous darkness of an old abandoned silver mine to find the long-lost loot from the 1902 Fort Hancock Payroll Robbery. And then they had to overcome multiple challenges and a serious injury, to make it back." She paused and glanced at each of them. "Now, my legal advisor has admonished me to be careful to qualify my enthusiasm, because this was a dangerous and risky endeavor—and I in no way would advise or condone anyone who doesn't know what they're doing to try and tackle what they did." She smiled and winked at her audience for effect. "But as a lover of adventure I just wanted to take the time this afternoon to celebrate them and give everyone here the opportunity to meet them personally."

There was another round of applause—spontaneous, this time. Then she continued. "Our friend, Justin Thyme from the *El Paso Border Report,* has interviewed each of them and put together a brief book about their exploits which you may purchase this afternoon if you like. Proceeds from the sales will go to our local Literacy & Libraries Foundation so it can continue its great work here in El Paso . . . So buy several!" Her laugh generated laughter in turn from her guests, who knew they'd been invited to a fundraiser and were prepared to buy multiple books as a donation to Sandra's favorite local charity.

"And, finally—don't forget that our adventurers will be happy to sign your book this afternoon." She paused while

Alex and Tyler headed back to where Eric was standing and Mac rejoined her girlfriends. Then she introduced and invited Principal Adams to join her. "This is Katie Adams, the principal at Alex, Tyler, and Mac's middle school. She's had a chance to hear more of this story, and has a presentation to make."

"Thank you, Sandra." Ms. Adams stepped forward to address the guests in her very loud and commanding principal's voice. "Our school received a very generous donation to our library this past week from Ms. Morrison-Parker. So first, let me say thank you, Sandra, for your interest in our kids. And second, I want everyone here to know that these three kids represent the bold, fearless, problem-solving mindset that excites us about the students in our school." There was a murmur of agreement from the crowd.

"Mac is not an experienced driver yet—you won't be seeing her on the roads for several more years, and yet she set aside her fears and focused on doing what needed to be done in order to rescue her uncle's fiancée, Jamie. As you'll see in Justin's book, she drove her uncle's Toyota Land Cruiser up a 25-degree rocky hillside and then along a narrow ledge at the upper edge of Rooster Canyon all by herself." She paused for some spontaneous applause and noise. "Then when she got back to the mine, she used the winch on that truck to free three hostages and rescue her family."

Mac's friends, Shaniyah, Monica, and Emme, leaned over to Mac and whispered loudly, "You go, Mac!"

"That's right!" Ms. Adams acknowledged, hearing the trio as they teased their friend. "You go, Mac!" and everyone broke into applause yet again. She resumed her comments. "And then there's Alex Ortiz, one of our superstars and a true computer guru." She looked over at Alex, who was standing with Madison on one side and Tyler on the other. "Alex is the one who figured out a puzzle and cryptogram that was over a hundred years old. When Mac's mom—Becky Foster—recognized a quote from Shakespeare's play *Macbeth* on the map, Alex immediately knew what kind of a code he was looking at and deciphered the cryptogram. Wow!"

Mac's friends now yelled, "Go, Alex!" and everyone applauded.

"And finally, our new student, Tyler. Earlier this summer, you may recall the story of his landing a plane when Eric, over there, had been kidnapped and drugged and was unable to fly. Tyler also was an important part of this adventure . . . Let's give it up for all three of these kids!"

Tyler, Mac, and Alex enjoyed the loud and long applause as they blushed and grinned at each other.

Now Sandra returned and thanked Ms. Adams. Then she got serious. "I have one last thing to share with you this afternoon, but before I do, I want to invite Mackenzie Foster—Mac, to join me again for just a moment." Sandra motioned Mac to come and stand with her.

"I know you'll all read about Mac's day in the desert and up at the Gunther-Morrison mine in Justin's book, but I couldn't let this afternoon go by without a special shout-out to a new, young hero of mine." Sandra smiled, looked Mac in the eyes, and nodded before she continued. "And that's precisely the word I want to use: *hero*. In my work over the years, I've made it a point to mentor women. Emerging executives, entrepreneurs, social and civic visionaries, and yes, I've also made a point of encouraging and assisting women who may be less well known but are having a tremendous impact on children, on other women, or on members of our society who need an advocate to simply stand alongside them in their need." Silent nods and subtle murmurs of agreement came from those guests who knew Sandra personally.

"Many of these women have gained my respect and admiration, and I'd go so far as to describe more than a few of them as heroes. I just want to point out that as I've had the chance to get to know Mackenzie these past few weeks and realize more fully what she really accomplished in spite of overwhelming odds, I find her to be an inspiration, an encouragement, and a reminder that being a hero is not a function of age or simple courage. It's a mindset that perseveres, that delivers an impactful result at a critical moment in time. So, let me invite you all to join me in calling out my new friend, one of my heroes—Mac and the young women like her—who will shape our world through their determination."

The audience created the loudest ovation Mac had ever heard. She felt overwhelmed as she graciously gave Sandra a quick hug, whispered thank you, and slipped back to join her girlfriends.

"Okay. Now, I have one last thing to share with all of you this afternoon." She turned again to face Alex, Mac, and Tyler. "As I mentioned a moment ago, I admire strong, focused people who can get things done. Each of our seven guests is already aware they're going to share a finder's reward. But today, I want to announce something special for Mac, Tyler, and Alex . . . I want to make certain they have the opportunity to pursue a higher education that matches each of their unique skills. Therefore, on behalf of the Morrison Family Trust and its interest in literacy and education, I'm presenting each of you with a scholarship account. Our board has agreed to underwrite your college expense at any school of your choosing after you graduate from high school." The crowd gave a collective gasp and then more applause.

Mac was amazed. She had overheard plenty of conversations between her parents about how expensive college is, so she understood what an incredible gift this was. Alex was stunned. He knew his mom was relying on him and his grades to get a scholarship when it came time to go to college—this removed that worry. Tyler wasn't sure what to think. He and his mom had never really talked about college so he'd assumed his dad would figure something out some day. Now he couldn't wait to tell him the news on their video call tonight. But he also wondered what it must be like to have so much money that you could just decide to pay for three kids to go to college. To be the focus of Miss Sandra's generosity almost felt overwhelming.

The rest of the afternoon was pretty much a blur for Tyler and Mac as they enjoyed answering questions from the dozens of guests who purchased books for them to sign. Alex and Tyler were excited for Mac that Sandra had asked her to work with the journalist on her special fund-raising project and all of them were impressed that her guests each made a $100 donation to her literacy fund for every copy of the book they signed.

Late in the afternoon, just before the party started to break up, Tyler was sitting by himself on the edge of the large stone fountain that was the centerpiece of the garden. Eric sat down beside him and said nothing for a couple of minutes, simply shared the view of the garden in silence. Then he spoke to his young friend; "I'm proud of you two, Tyler. You're both amazing kids, and neither of you has let things go to your head. You got the kudos earlier this summer—well-deserved, I might add. But this time Mac's in the spotlight and she looks like she's handling all the attention pretty well too."

"Well, she deserves it," Tyler responded after thinking a moment. "I couldn't have done what she did. I'd have killed the clutch or driven off the ledge." He looked at Eric, grinned, and corrected himself. "Actually, I probably wouldn't have driven off the edge . . . but she sure knew what she was doing getting the Cruiser up that hill."

Eric nodded and was quiet again, inspecting a bed of flowering yucca in the late afternoon light. "But you know what's exciting for me?"

"What's that?"

"Seeing you both step up and do things that no one else would have bet you could do. It's surprising and rewarding at the same time."

"Feels kind of cool, actually," Tyler nodded.

"And it should, Tyler. Doing something big should always bring a personal sense of satisfaction." He paused for a moment and neither of them spoke. "When I was in the army, I had the chance to see a lot of heroes."

"I can just imagine."

"You know what they all had in common? Instinct. It's not that they intended to do something heroic. They just did what they did with intent. They'd already decided somehow that they weren't going to let fear of failure define their choices."

"How so?"

"Well, I guess my point is that being a hero isn't something you set out to do. It's how other people end up seeing the way you did something—something you instinctively knew you needed to do when it had to be done. Something that another person might have failed to try because they let their fears get the best of them."

Tyler thought about that for a moment. "Yeah, I can see that."

"So, anyway, you get credit in my book for sticking with me and Ryan and Jamie in that dark mine shaft and for not freaking out or abandoning Jamie. You and Mac, you're both heroes in my book, Tyler Dubois."

"Kinda strange to say it out loud," Tyler said, smiling at Eric, "but I was pretty proud of Mac myself."

"Well, save that thought, my friend. Make sure you tell her that soon. She might act embarrassed, but it would mean a lot to her to hear you tell her that."

After Eric left, Tyler looked around and spotted Mac. She was hanging out with her girlfriends, who were treating her like a rock star. If Mac had freaked out and given up, things might have turned out very differently. But she did what she knew how to do and kept after it even when things didn't look so good— and it made a difference. He thought about telling her now, but realized that she was having too much fun. He'd be sure to talk to her tonight when they were home . . . maybe over a bowl of Bluebell ice cream.

He got up, stretched, and scanned the garden. *Time to go find Alex.*

AUTHOR'S NOTE

The events in this story are fictitious. The characters are not real, nor are they intended to reflect any living individual. As mentioned in my first book, *Sky High Danger*, I acknowledge that certain liberties have been taken in the process of storytelling. I know there's a range of mountains to the southeast of El Paso and just north of the small border town of Fort Hancock, which is just off I-10. There is not, however, a Rooster Canyon within those mountains as far as I know, nor any active or past silver mines. However, considerable silver mining went on in New Mexico in the nineteenth century and there was also some limited silver mining near El Paso where these stories are set. As for the loan shark and the professor, the wire taps, and the FBI, these portrayals are my inventions for the fun of a good story and are not based on any known actual events.

Finally, I would note that my youngest daughter and I had a close encounter with a large rattlesnake in a desert brush setting years ago and cannot recommend it. Such a near miss is frightening and potentially very dangerous. If you intend to go out into the desert, (or other wild places . . .) please be careful!

ACKNOWLEDGMENTS

Writing a story is a big task that takes time and most importantly is fed by the inspiration and encouragement of friends and family. Anita (my wife) and I sat at dinner in Victoria, BC, a couple of years ago after finalizing the manuscript for my first book. I was puzzling what our new cast of characters might take on in Book Two of this series.

As we talked, I suggested the time-honored adventure theme of a treasure hunt or lost silver mine. She pulled out her cell phone, did a quick search, and noted that there had, in fact, been a few silver mines near El Paso in the 1800s. Then and there we began crafting the essential framework for this second book. Anita has been my lifelong muse and I thank her for reading and commenting and encouraging me throughout all my projects.

My brother, Chris, has once more played an instrumental role in both inspiration, encouragement, and initial read-throughs. He also applied his graphic arts skills in the layout and typesetting, and again, produced the cover art. Thanks, so much, Chris!

The legal framework of who owns lost treasure is critically important for a story like this to be believable—even if it is fictitious. Brandon Marx (my son-in-law) is a lawyer and provided me with the research and legal theory to accurately build the story's closing chapters. Thanks, Brandon!

A friend with a large ranch near Burnet, Texas took me around his property in his old Jeep CJ one afternoon, scaling steep embankments in four-low as we explored his place. That, unfortunately, is the extent of my 4WD off-roading experience. To better understand the true challenges that Mac would have faced in her "impossible task," I turned to James Alexander, an off-roading, 4WD enthusiast with significant back trail experience in Texas and Idaho. I appreciate his willingness to help me better describe Mac's experience in the driver's seat of the Toyota FJ40. Thanks again, James!

Let me note that when one is stepping into a new craft, it helps to have a lot of feedback and particularly to have early readers who can offer frank, creative input . . . even if that input means reconsidering chapters and plot lines you thought were complete. Besides my brother Chris, his wife—Kelley Owen— served as an early reader. Importantly, Kelley was a big advocate for the character of Mac as it evolved in this second book and helped shape Mac's emotional experiences. (Kelley will know the chapter that is uniquely based on her recommendation!) Thanks, Kelley!

And last, but certainly not least, my sincere appreciation to Sandy Chapman for agreeing once more to be my editor. As a relatively new author, it is so encouraging to work with a talented, seasoned professional. She too was a big champion on behalf of Mackenzie and I truly appreciate her investment in Mac's character development in this story. Once again, thank you so much, Sandy!

Finally, let me just say that writing is both hard work and great fun. If you have a story to tell, for goodness sake, get started telling it!

Dave Owen

Lightning Source UK Ltd.
Milton Keynes UK
UKHW011847070121
376641UK00001B/93